GHOSTS & LEGENDS
OF THE CAROLINA COASTS

GHOSTS & LEGENDS

OF THE CAROLINA COASTS

Terrance Zepke

ILLUSTRATED BY MICHAEL SWING

PINEAPPLE PRESS, INC.
SARASOTA, FLORIDA

Inquiries should be addressed to:

Pineapple Press, Inc.
P.O. Box 3889
Sarasota, Florida 34230

www.pineapplepress.com

Library of Congress Cataloging-in-Publication Data

Zepke, Terrance,
  Ghosts & legends of the Carolina coasts / Terrance Zepke.—1st ed.
    p. cm.
  Includes bibliographical references.
  ISBN-13: 978-1-56164-336-3 (pbk. : alk. paper)
  1. Ghosts—North Carolina—Atlantic Coast. 2. Ghosts—South Carolina—
Atlantic Coast. I. Title: Ghosts and legends of the Carolina coasts. II. Title.
  BF1472.U6Z457 2005
  133.1'09756'09146—dc22
                                                          2005019459

First Edition
10 9 8 7 6 5 4 3

Printed in the United States of America

North Carolina

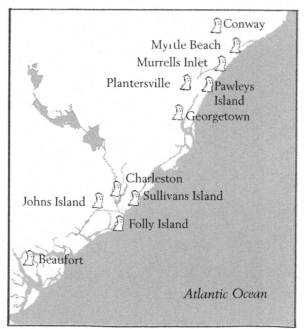

South Carolina

CONTENTS

INTRODUCTION

*T*his is not my first ghost book; nor is it my second, or even my third. This is my fourth book on ghosts of the Carolinas. You may wonder what compels a person to write numerous ghost books. There are several reasons for this compulsion. One is that I absolutely love ghost stories. I remember my college professors drilling into my head "write what you love," so that is what I've done.

Our legends help preserve the history and heritage of the Carolinas. By knowing them, we get a rare glimpse into what these communities and their inhabitants were like once upon a time. Towns that no longer exist, or at the very least have changed drastically, and lifestyles that long ago became extinct, are revealed. For example, lifesaving stations with heroic crews, active (and remote) lighthouses and their keepers, nefarious pirates, salt of the earth lightering pilots and whalers were once an intrinsic part of our coasts.

I also love the thrill that each bizarre tale brings us. I get goose bumps when I hear what has happened to the night watchman aboard the USS *North Carolina* in "Sailor Spirits." Vivid images of watery graves and outstretched hands flash before my eyes when I close them and recall "Ship of Fire." My heart breaks when I think about the wreck of the *Crissie Wright* and all the lives that were lost that night. How helpless those on shore must have felt as they watched the crew, one by one, slowly give in to their horrific fate!

I am reminded of the terrible things sometimes done in the name of love when I think about the "Spirit of Poor Nell Cropsey," "Secret Signal," "Brown Lady of Chowan College," and "Haunted Hammock House."

A chill runs down my spine when I think about strange, inexplicable things like "Ghostly Hoofprints," "And the Sea Will Tell," and "Colonel Buck's Curse." I dare the naysayers to provide me with any plausible scientific explanation! Those stories affect me the most because there is no rational explanation to dismiss what has been witnessed.

However, I can't help smiling when I think about "Hatteras Jack" and "Calling the *Real* Gray Man." Thank goodness for them. I like that there are no simple explanations for them. We can use all the help we can get, regardless of what benevolent form it takes—even an albino dolphin or gray-cloaked ghost!

Some stories, such as "Pirate Specter," "Drunken Jack," and "Dram Tree Superstition" conjure up images of diehard, rum-swigging buccaneers and their outlandish seafaring traditions.

I don't know about anyone else, but I am glad there are some things that cannot be readily explained. The world is a better place with a few juicy mysteries and good, old-fashioned "read with the lights on" scary ghost stories and legends.

I hope you'll visit my web site, www.terrancezepke.com, and let me know which stories you enjoyed the most. Did any of them keep you awake most of the night? Did you have trouble getting one of them out of your mind? If you visited one of the haunted places mentioned in this book, did you find yourself looking over your shoulder? Did a chill come over you as you walked into the room of a reportedly haunted place? Or perhaps you know a story that I have not yet heard that you'd like to share.

Maybe we'll meet sometime while exploring the same haunted place and we can swap tales of ghostly encounters.

Dear, beauteous death, the jewel of the just!
Shining nowhere but in the dark;
What mysteries do lie beyond thy dust,
Could man outlook that mark!

— Henry Vaughan
1622–1695

The captain and his men murdered every passenger. Next, they loaded the loot onto the lifeboats and set the ship on fire to hide any proof of their crime.

S tand watch, Simmons, and give a call if anyone approaches," the captain ordered.

"All right, now, listen up," he commanded his men, who were huddled around their leader waiting for his announcement. "These poor people, these Palatines, we've been carrying across the ocean ain't poor at all. They're been holding out on us."

"I don't believe it, sir," said one of the men.

"Are you calling me a liar?" growled the captain.

"Why, uh, no. No, sir. I just mean why would they pretend to be poor?" he asked incredulously.

The captain and his first mate looked at each other and nearly doubled over with laughter. "Have you got a thing or two to learn!" the captain proclaimed. Both men had been pirates before accepting the King's Pardon, an agreement between a pirate and the Crown that said the Crown would forgive all past acts of piracy if the pirate in question swore never to perform another one. While many felt compelled to accept the pardon rather than end up jailed or hanged, they also had a hard time returning to a law-abiding lifestyle. They needed only the smallest excuse to slip back into their old ways.

The first mate said, "They're pretending to be poor so we don't steal all their riches, get it?"

"With all due respect, sir, how do we know they have riches?" another crewman asked.

"We know because I said so!" roared the captain. "We also know because shortly after Dutch called 'Land ho!' they came up on deck with bags laden down with silver candlesticks, good china, coins, fine clothes, and jewelry."

Every one of his men gaped at their leader with open mouths and awed expressions.

"But captain, sir, they'll never just hand over their possessions to us," said a senior crewmember.

"No, I don't expect they'll give up their precious possessions without a struggle," agreed the captain. "That's why we have to be prepared to kill every last one of them!"

The men sat in silence for a good minute before the first mate suggested they vote on it. "Say 'aye' if you want to be rich beyond your wildest dreams," he said.

The room was filled with "Aye" being shouted loud and clear. "Okay, now let me hear 'Nay' if you want to land and put the Palatines ashore with all their belongings," the first mate said.

"Nay!" "Nay!"

"All right. The ayes have it. We proceed with our plan," said the captain.

All ships had to clear customs, and Ocracoke was a major port of entry. The process usually took a couple of hours and then the ship got under way for its final destination. In this case, the ship's final destination was New Bern, North Carolina. The Palatines had gathered their belongings to take ashore while the ship was inspected and any duties paid. That is when the "loot" was discovered.

In accordance with their new plan, the captain informed the Palatines that the tide was against them, so it would be impossible to navigate the tricky Ocracoke Inlet. They would have to wait until early the next morning to go ashore. The group was very disappointed but could do nothing about the bad news. They took their belongings and returned to their cabins. The captain put his trusted first mate in charge of getting rid of any lightering boats. Lightering pilots were local men who knew the waters like the back of their hands. They helped large vessels transverse the shallow inlets, sounds, and shoals.

The Palatines were murdered in their sleep by the captain and his men—not a single passenger was left alive. Then the crew loaded the loot onto the lifeboats and set the ship on fire to hide any proof of their crime. They rowed to shore, looking back frequently to see if the ocean had engulfed the burning vessel. Instead, it just kept burning. And then the men thought their eyes must have been playing tricks on them because the ship began to sail! It continued to burn as it bobbed on the water.

The captain and his men arrived ashore and continued to watch the spectacle. It burned all night but was still floating around the mouth of the Neuse River. Impossible! Legend has it that on the anniversary of this tragic night the Fire Ship of New Bern can be seen here. For one night it burns and floats, then it disappears until the next year. Look for her on the first night of a new moon during September. The smell of fire and the sound of plaintive wailing accompany the ship.

As is only fitting, it is said that the men were spooked by the fire ship and believed it was a sign that the gods were very angry at their villainous acts. They hid out in the forest, using their money to buy what they needed, but not enjoying their wealth very much. Some believe that the Ship of Fire will continue to blaze until retribution is made on behalf of the men, women, and children who were savagely murdered aboard the ship.

I have also heard this story called "The Flaming Ship of Oc-

The Palatines of New Bern

The religious wars between the Protestants and Catholics had caused serious damage to Germany, homeland of the Palatines. Most of their fertile farmland and homes were destroyed. Approximately ten thousand Palatine refugees went to England, but the British didn't know what to do with them. The large population jeopardized the British economy. Swiss Baron Christopher Von Graffenried, who by some accounts was also a Palatine, proposed taking several hundred of them to the New World and suggested a place called Carolina. Queen Anne was delighted—the idea of more British colonists appealed to her, and she eagerly said yes. The first group to be relocated took whatever valuables they still had and headed to America. Their land and homes may have been annihilated, but these fine craftsmen and miners had many family heirlooms that were, collectively, worth a great deal of money.

New Bern is the second oldest town in North Carolina and because of this boasts more than one hundred historic sites. Baron Christopher Von Graffenreid settled it in 1710, when he purchased the land from the Tuscarora Indians. The town, which was named for the city of Bern, Switzerland, is situated where the Trent and Neuse Rivers meet.

Union forces captured New Bern on March 14, 1862. Officers and soldiers occupied several residences throughout the war. Some were turned into headquarters and hospitals. For this reason, many dwellings are on the National Register of Historic Places and reportedly haunted.

SAILOR SPIRITS

Bradshaw wanted out of there, but he wasn't about to go in that direction . . . he began climbing the ladder . . . He stopped when he heard something overhead banging, followed by the shuffling of feet.

W ilmington, North Carolina is full of haunted places, including Thalian Hall, Burgwin-Wright House, and the USS *North Carolina* Battleship. This haunted battle-ship is now permanently moored at Eagles Island on the scenic Cape Fear River.

Until recently, the fact that it was haunted was one of the best-kept secrets in Wilmington. The reason for this was that only one man, night watchman Danny Bradshaw, has been aboard the ship after hours for the last thirty years. Bradshaw has access to restricted areas of the ship and is the only human being aboard it much of the time, which means he has the greatest chance of seeing ghosts.

Bradshaw's claim is difficult to validate for the same reason. However, he invited a serious amateur ghost-hunting group to investigate in the hopes of doing just that. A team from Seven Paranormal Research, armed with an array of ghost detecting devices such as motion detectors and temperature sensors, spent several hours exploring the retired warship on February 21, 2004. Seven Paranormal Research was a private organization, but according to their web site (http://www.hauntednc.com) are now a 501(c)3 (nonprofit) organization. The group has been in existence for fourteen years, and during that time it has investigated many strange phenomena and paranormal incidents.

The ghost hunters poked around the most likely places on the ship, which Bradshaw said were the port bow, engine room, sick bay, and mess hall. The night watchman says that doors and hatches open and close by themselves, and sometimes lights and televisions turn on and off on their own. Footsteps and voices can be heard, but no one is there. Additionally, cold spots have been felt and objects have inexplicably been moved. According to Bradshaw, sometimes several ghostly events occur within a short amount of time, and sometimes nothing extraordinary takes place for months.

Although the ghosts didn't reveal themselves to the Seven Paranormal Research investigators, and the team's audio and vibration monitors were rendered useless due to the continuous creaking and rolling of the massive metal ship, Bradshaw maintains that there are ghosts. In fact, he has written a book about them called *Ghosts on the Battleship North Carolina*. In the book, Bradshaw explains that ten crew members died aboard this vessel during World War II. Five of the men died when a Japanese missile hit the front of the ship on September 15, 1942. Three more were killed by friendly fire in April 1945. The other men died in two separate incidents. Bradshaw theorizes that the men were so young when they died that they might not have been able to accept their fate.

"If there are any tortured souls onboard who might believe they died too young, it's probably these guys," Bradshaw told Associated Press during an interview. The night watchman has actually seen the ghosts of young navy sailors. He says their presence usually doesn't bother him "but a few times I've felt a cold and evil feeling."

It started when Bradshaw took over the job after a friend of his, who had held the position for five years, left to pursue another career. The friend assured him it was an easy job but cautioned, "There are going to be things that happen here that there's no explanation for." Some people think it's funny and want Bradshaw to take them aboard the haunted ship, but he says, "I want you to understand this place is haunted. I get scared. I get horrified."

The first time he saw a ghost, Bradshaw was on his way to the galley during his nightly rounds. He had to use his flashlight to go from power switch to power switch because the lights are turned off at night for economy. As his beam cut through the darkness, it revealed sailors standing in line for meal service. While their faces were vague, there was no mistaking that these were uniformed men. Next he felt cold air and a hand on his shoulder! He quickly turned around, but saw nothing. He did, however, hear footsteps, as if someone were walking away.

Bradshaw surveyed the rest of the room with his flashlight. He nearly with fainted with fear at what he saw. A young blond sailor stood in an open hatch. "It was the horrible-est thing I've ever experienced," Bradshaw says. Bradshaw wanted out of there, but he wasn't about to go in that direction. Instead, he began climbing the ladder to the next deck. He stopped when he heard something overhead banging, followed by the shuffling of feet.

"I lost it," he says. "I thought, 'he's not going to let me out.'" Bradshaw nearly fell off the ladder in his haste to get down. Then he ran back through the other side of the ship to another set of ladders, praying he would be able to escape. His prayers were answered, and he got out of there without further incident.

Bradshaw believes that at least two of the men who died aboard the ship still haunt it. He says that one is harmless—he just likes to slam doors, move objects, and turn off lights. The other ghost, Bradshaw feels, is pure evil. The room gets very cold, indicating his presence. Bradshaw hears footsteps coming up behind him as if running to attack him, and sometimes the ghost yells as he approaches. However, the watchman has learned not to scream or run. If he does nothing, the ghost goes away.

"All of a sudden, you start getting an eerie feeling, like something bad is going to happen." Both ghosts typically harass him for several minutes before disappearing. Bradshaw also says that the ghosts have revealed themselves to other employees, visitors touring the ship, and friends that he has invited aboard.

*Photo courtesy of North Carolina Division of Tourism,
Film, and Sports Development*

USS *North Carolina*

USS *North Carolina* Battleship was commissioned in 1941 and used during World War II to protect aircraft carriers. The warship participated in every major naval offense that occurred in the Pacific Theater. She accommodated approximately 2,300 crew members, was involved in every significant offensive of the WWII, and earned fifteen battle stars during her tenure. The *North Carolina* was considered one of the fastest and most worthy warships in the world. The vessel was decommissioned in 1947 and was nearly scrapped, but North Carolinians swung into action. Their "Save Our Ship" campaign not only spared the great old vessel from becoming scrap metal, it also brought the retired warship back to North Carolina. It had been stored in the Inactive Reserve Fleet in New Jersey. Since April 1962 the ship has served as a World War II memorial.

The *North Carolina* is on Eagles Island, which was named in honor of Richard Eagles, an area planter. During the eighteenth century, the island produced large quantities of rice, which was exported via the Wilmington harbor. The battleship, which was brought to the area by Captain B. M. Burris, sits on the New Hanover-Brunswick County line.

The 40,000-ton, nine-deck ship is open daily for self-guided tours. There is a shipboard museum, which includes a "Roll of Honor" list of all North Carolina men who died during World War II, as well as a snack bar, gift shop, large parking lot, and picnic area. Tours and special events are offered throughout the year. The ship can even be rented for special occasions. It can accommodate groups of up to 350 people.

The island is located at the junction of Highways 17, 74, 76, and 421, which is across from Wilmington's Historic District. Take the Cape Fear Memorial Bridge out of Wilmington. Eagles Island is linked to the mainland by a causeway. The ship is just across the bridge on the right. Or hire the water taxi, which departs from the foot of Market Street.

For more information call 910-251-5797 or 350-1817, or visit the web site, www.battleshipnc.com. There is a special section for educators, "Teacher Resources."

TWO LINGERING

Servants have discovered that rocker moving back and forth of its own accord. They also report an eerie feeling that sometimes comes over them when they enter that room.

Georgetown, South Carolina, is a thriving place filled with boaters traveling along the Intracoastal Waterway and day-trippers who drive to the scenic port town in order to enjoy its historic district. Georgetown is situated on the Atlantic Ocean where the Waccamaw, Black, Sampit, and Pee Dee Rivers meet to form Winyah Bay. It began as a Spanish settlement in 1526, but was later abandoned because of a fever epidemic. The British settled there in 1700, and the first land grant was issued in 1705. The first parish, Prince George, was granted in 1722 to Baptist minister Elisha Screven, and it was recognized as an official port in 1729. It was five more years before this parish officially became Georgetown, so named after England's King George II. It became the third oldest port in the state. After the Revolutionary War, indigo plantations gave way to rice production. The Lowcountry, with its many rivers, was perfect for growing rice. By 1840, Georgetown County produced half of the rice grown in the United States. In fact, it exported more rice than any other port in the world. Until the Civil War, beautiful rice plantations lined what is now the Intracoastal Waterway.

During the city's heyday as one of the largest rice exporters in the world, the 550-acre Prospect Hill Plantation was created. It was later owned by Mary Allston, who was widowed in 1794. The widow remarried Benjamin Huger, Jr., a politician who served in the South Carolina Senate, South Carolina House of Representatives, and the United States Congress during his illustrious career.

Mary was again widowed in 1823, which left the burden of running the plantation on her shoulders. She loved Prospect Hill and fulfilled her role well until she came down with a debilitating disease several years later. Ultimately, she was nearly bedridden, but she often sat on the lovely covered porch and walkway that was located just outside her bedroom, which afforded her a great view of the plantation she so loved.

When she passed away in 1838, the plantation's five hundred slaves sang and prayed in her honor. Miss Mary had always been good to them and she would be greatly missed. Through the years since then, slaves, residents, and guests of Prospect Hill have seen a woman wearing a white nightgown on the porch where the plantation mistress had spent so much time.

Remarkably, the ghost of Mary Allston is not the only spirit that lingers at Prospect Hill. After her death, Colonel Joshua Ward bought the plantation. When he died in 1852, one of his sons inherited it. Unfortunately, it wasn't much of a gift—rice plantations never returned to the pre–Civil War days of production. This meant they generated less income than operating expenses. The young man needed a loan to keep the plantation going, so he made a trip to Charleston. Sadly, no banker would extend the desperate planter any further credit. Ward went to a bar and tried to drink his troubles away. His judgment clouded, he joined in a card game hoping he could win some money. Instead, he lost every cent he had. The depressed man returned to the plantation and continued to drink. Unable to face his failure, he took his own life.

His body was found on the floor by his favorite rocker with a gun in his outstretched hand. On many occasions, servants have discovered that rocker moving back and forth of its own accord. They also report an eerie feeling that sometimes comes over them when they enter that room. The most telling encounter, however, took place soon after Ward's suicide. The new mistress of the plantation chose Joshua Ward's former bedroom as her own. One night, soon after she was settled in the room, a man appeared in front of her wearing well-made but well-worn clothing, and holding a pistol. He has been seen numerous times since then. Many people believe that this is the spirit of Joshua Ward. According to many eyewitnesses, the spirits of both Miss Mary and Joshua Ward roamed Prospect Hill for many years. The former plantation, also known as Arcadia Plantation, is located about five miles from Georgetown on the Waccamaw River. The Georgian-style structure has been on the National Register of Historic Places since 1978. It is privately owned and I have been unable to find out if it is still haunted.

Georgetown

In its early days, the city of Georgetown, South Carolina, was dependent on indigo and rice plantations. Later, lumber production became an important industry—Georgetowr ̶ ̶ ̶ ̶
lumberyard on the East Coast. The Internation
set up operation there in 1936 and by 1944 ·
ployer in the county. At the end of World W:
were sold to land developers who subdivided
tourism and commercial fishing have repl:
production. This scenic waterfront comm
among the top one hundred small towns ir
wish to explore the Kaminski House M
or take a tour of the city. For more infoɾ
Georgetown Visitor's Center at 843-54(

WAILING AT

Skeletal remains were found inside large burial urns, which were also arranged in a circle.

Among the many splendid rice plantations built in the Georgetown, South Carolina, area during the eighteenth century was Wachesaw Plantation. It is widely believed that the word *Wachesaw* originated with the Waccamaw Indians and it means "Place of Great Weeping." This makes sense because the area was an Indian burial ground before the planters took possession.

The first Wachesaw planter was John Allston, who came in 1733. Reverend James Belin assumed ownership in 1825. The Methodist minister ran the plantation and five mission churches until his carriage violently overturned on Wachesaw Road, killing him almost instantly.

Reverend Belin's nephew, Allard Belin Flagg, inherited the plantation. Dr. Flagg tore down the Church of St. John, which was part of Wachesaw Plantation property; the edifice had deteriorated during the Civil War, and Flagg decided to salvage what lumber he could to build a summer home at what is now Garden City. Some folks, including former Wachesaw slaves who were then employed by the plantation, strongly advised against this idea. No good would come of demolishing the Lord's house, they warned, and suggested that he give serious thought to renovating the old church rather than destroying it. However, Allard Flagg wasn't the kind of man who listened to others, especially when their ideas conflicted with his own. Instead, he painstakingly removed the best lumber and proceeded to build a handsome cottage, which was destroyed by a storm almost before it was finished. Flagg doggedly rebuilt the house, and again it was annihilated by a storm as soon as construction was completed. After that, Flagg abandoned his plan.

The original Wachesaw Plantation home caught fire and burned to the ground in 1890. In the early 1900s, the family sold the property. In 1930 a wealthy New Yorker named William Kimbel bought it for hunting. An Indian burial ground, which contained thirteen skeletons laid out in a circle, was discovered during construction of his hunting lodge.

In 1937, work began on Kimbel's home, and another Indian burial ground was unearthed during construction. Skeletal remains were found inside large burial urns, which were also arranged in a circle. Most of the skeletons from both sites were women and children. One theory about the cause of their deaths was that they contracted diphtheria from European traders. Beads and other trinkets found on and with the skeletons supported this theory.

The remains and relics were taken to the Charleston Museum for additional analysis. Some workers stole relics from the dig, either to keep as souvenirs or to sell for profit. The artifacts would fetch good money, they reasoned. One man who kept four or five relics was awakened the first night he brought them home by a pitiful wailing. The disturbing cries were followed by the appearance of an Indian brave, who was standing over the relics the thief had placed on a table near his bed. This same eerie scene happened every night for more than a week. Exhausted and frightened, the man finally returned the items to the museum. Legend has it that other workers who had stolen relics had similar experiences. They, too, returned the items and never heard the wailing or saw the Indian brave again.

The former plantation, located nineteen miles north of Georgetown near Murrells Inlet, is now Wachesaw Landing. William Kimbel's home and hunting lodge were torn down in 1985 to make room for this residential community. Area residents claim that they still hear wailing from time to time at the former burial site. Skeptics say it is just the wind "wailing wildly." Or could it be the spirits of Wachesaw women and children crying out as they succumbed to diphtheria?

DRUNKEN JACK

They sang and drank and carried on partying for the better part of the night.

The infamous pirate Blackbeard sailed all around the Carolinas. He plundered merchant ships, drank in waterfront taverns, and even settled down briefly in North Carolina. There are dozens of legends pertaining to this swashbuckler. One that South Carolina Lowcountry residents are proud to tell is about Blackbeard and Drunken Jack. According to legend, Blackbeard raided a merchant ship in the Caribbean that held so much rum he could neither consume it all nor carry the weight. In reality, the pirates probably didn't want to be caught with all that rum. It would be obvious they had stolen it and they would be arrested. What's more, the liquor was too good to quickly consume or sell for half its value just to be rid of it.

So Blackbeard and his men put in at a deserted island adjacent to Murrells Inlet. They had used the place before, and were therefore confident their rum would be safe. They buried all but what they needed to throw a good party. The men caught oysters and roasted them—delicious! They went well with Jamaica's finest rum. They sang and drank and carried on partying for the better part of the night, and one by one the pirates passed out.

One of Blackbeard's crew, a young man named Jack, sought a comfortable spot away from the blazing fire and diehard revelers. He fell fast asleep under a palmetto. When he awoke, his head felt like it was going to explode—what a hangover! Jack lay there a long time trying to clear his head. After a while, he realized it was far too quiet for an island filled with pirates. The buccaneer eventually managed to rouse himself to have a look around. He wobbled for a minute or two, steadied himself, and slowly made his way over the sand dunes. He couldn't believe what he saw on the other side.

There were no pirates! The ship was gone, and they had sailed without him. About the same time that Jack realized what had happened, crew members noticed Jack missing. A thorough search of the ship revealed he was not aboard. "We must have left him on the island," the first mate informed Blackbeard. "Should we turn back, sir?"

"No! We're nearly a day away. We'd lose two days and risk getting caught by the British Navy. We'll be back there sooner or later. Jack can take care of himself."

The man nodded his agreement. They had barely eluded the military, which was how they ended up at Murrells Inlet in the first place. It would be foolhardy to go back. Besides, who had ever disagreed with Blackbeard and lived to tell about it?

One version of the tale has it that the pirates couldn't get back because it was too risky. War had broken out and the waters were filled with battleships. If that were true, it would have been dangerous to travel from the Caribbean to the Carolinas. It may also have been that they got distracted with all the good plunder and partying that the Caribbean provided. The abandoned pirate was probably not at the top of Blackbeard's list of priorities. Whatever the reason, it was a year or so before the pirates returned to fetch Jack and their rum. If they hadn't buried thirty-two cases of premium rum on the island, I dare say they would have never returned for poor Jack.

What they found was a mystery. All the rum bottles were empty, and instead of their fellow pirate they discovered a skeleton. Were these the remains of Jack or some other unfortunate soul? There might have been no doubt that it was Drunken Jack, except that a buried treasure chest had been dug up and taken away. Only Jack would have known where it was. Perhaps another band of pirates happened along and Jack negotiated his passage off the island by revealing the exact location of the buried treasure; if that was the case, it seems that the sea robbers didn't want to share any of it with Jack, so they left him behind once again. Or perhaps someone just happened to stumble upon it after finding the dead pirate.

The island remains uninhabited. Some residents say the spirit of Drunken Jack lives on. His name certainly does, at least: Drunken Jack's is a popular waterfront restaurant with a view of Drunken Jack's Island. The back of their menu includes a condensed version of this legend.

Murrells Inlet

Murrells Inlet is an old fishing village that was founded in the late eighteenth century by Captain Morrall. It is renowned for its Gulf Stream deep-sea fishing. Business Highway 17 runs through Murrells Inlet and is lined with tourist businesses, including Drunken Jack's Restaurant and Bar. Drunken Jack Island is inside the south jetty, just behind the north end of Huntington Beach. It can be seen just to the right of the inlet if you're on the gazebo of the Hot Fish Club (4911 Hwy. 17 Business) or on the deck of Russell's Seafood Grill and Raw Bar (South Murrells Inlet).

RAM TREE

SUPERSTITION

Departing sailors gathered around the tree, opened the good rum, and drank a toast to their safe voyage.

*T*here once stood a grand cypress tree that was on the waterfront at Edenton's harbor. Legend has it the huge tree existed before the first settlers arrived at the New World. Sailors, who are generally supposed to be superstitious and fond of traditions, began leaving a bottle of Jamaican run in a hollow part of the tree's trunk when they arrived in port. Departing sailors gathered around the tree, opened the good rum, and drank a toast to their safe voyage. As word spread, seamen always stopped at the Dram Tree to do their "duty."

Those who failed to leave a bottle of rum upon their safe arrival or failed to partake of the traditional rum toast before departure soon regretted their mistake. These captains and their crews suffered terrible storms, and sometimes the men didn't survive. One ship reportedly sank before it even got out of the harbor! The first mate had told his captain only an hour earlier that the vessel was "as seaworthy as any ship on the waters, sir." In his haste to set sail—or perhaps he may have been one of the few seamen who wasn't superstitious—the captain skipped the tradition and hurriedly set sail. After the ship sank for no apparent reason, the captain always participated in a good luck drink at the Dram Tree.

The men who didn't partake in a good luck toast also encountered calm seas that stranded them for days, or even weeks, in the midst of the ocean, with nothing more to do than to pray for wind to carry them on their way.

In 1917, a large mass of ice formed on top of the water due to a harsh winter. When the spring of 1918 arrived, the formation melted and the Dram Tree was destroyed. This unfortunately ended the tradition.

Edenton

Over the years, several hurricanes have affected this area, and many waterfront homes suffered extensive damage. Flooding has occurred on many occasions. Nonetheless, Edenton is a quaint waterfront town that deserves its nickname, "The South's Prettiest Little Town."

Edenton, established in 1690, is one of the oldest towns in the state and among the oldest in the United States. It was incorporated in 1715 as "the Towne on Queen Anne's Creek." The name was later changed to Edenton in honor of former North Carolina Governor Charles Eden. Its residents have had a hand in shaping our history, from Joseph Hewes, who signed the Declaration of Independence, to Hugh Williamson, who signed the U. S. Constitution.

Angry Gods and Albatrosses

There are as many superstitions involving the sea as there are coastal ghosts. For instance, did you know that thunder, lightning, and fierce winds have been thought to be manifestations of the anger of the gods? If someone was struck by lightning, shipwrecked, or drowned at sea, it was because the gods were angry. Another superstition involves the albatross, which was thought to herald bad wind and foul weather if it circled around a ship in mid-ocean. It was very unlucky to harm an albatross, because it was thought to embody the restless spirit of a dead mariner.

Bell Baruch had heard the stories about the ghost of Thomas Young and decided that the original building and ghost story would add a certain charm to her new home.

*H*ave you ever wanted something so badly that you couldn't rest until you got it? Thomas Young did—he wanted a house that trumped all other Georgetown, South Carolina, plantation homes. His home would have the best view, the grandest entry, and the most ornate woodwork. He had already come across the beginnings of such a house on his property. Two long, brick chimneys protruded from the foundation. He didn't know who had started the construction or why it had been stopped, but this spot certainly possessed the best view of Winyah Bay and was a good start for his home.

In order to finance such a dream house, Young would have to cultivate more rice than he had originally anticipated. So he began clearing more swampland. This was a terrible task, as you can probably imagine. He supervised the slaves as they cut through thick vegetation that had grown wild for many years. He directed them as they chopped down trees. The project was moving forward, slowly but surely.

One day he heard that President Washington might visit this area the following year. Wouldn't that be something if the president chose to come to Thomas Young's home instead of Billy Alston's? Currently, Billy Alston's Clifton Plantation was the grandest of all the area homes, but if Thomas Young could get his magnificent dwelling up before next year there would be little doubt that President Washington would be sitting at his table instead!

So Young had some of his slaves start building the house. Meanwhile, the swampland was still being turned into rice fields. If the work wasn't done in the next couple of months, they would be unable to plant the seeds this year, which would mean that there would be no rice harvest to pay the bills. The stress was enormous. Poor Thomas Young ran himself ragged going back and forth from the rice fields to the construction site. He was up before sunrise and working until well after sunset. When the slaves were dismissed, Young, carrying a lantern, walked through the house and inspected every detail of that day's construction.

One morning he was so tired he overslept. When he realized the time, he quickly dressed and hurried to the rice fields. Once satisfied that everyone was doing what they were supposed to be doing and that there were no problems that required his attention, Young proceeded to his dream house. He raced around pointing out things that needed to be corrected and reassigning some men to different tasks. At the end of the day, the overworked man was so tired he could barely make it home. He didn't even have the energy to inspect that day's work. Young went to bed as soon as he got home. He never woke up.

Work on the house stopped after the death of Thomas Young, and eventually his neighbor Billy Alston bought the land. Soon thereafter, he received a letter notifying him that President Washington was coming to dine at Clifton. The night after the president was entertained by Billy Alston, a figure, which seemed to be the ghost of Thomas Young, was seen carrying a lantern through the

Young house. It stopped often and held up the light as if inspecting the woodwork.

The slaves swore a plat-eye haunted the house. A plat-eye was considered to be worse than a ghost. It was an evil entity that took over the bodies of animals such as dogs, cats, and wolves. A slave named Mattie recalled she once saw a white cat turn into a big, white dog that had red eyes. A runaway slave was supposedly so frightened by the sight of the specter that he ran back to his master! A white owl made its home in the half-built house, so it came to be known as White Owl House for a while. Some people say they have seen two figures—an apparition holding a lantern showing the house to a ghostly guest. There has been speculation that perhaps this is Thomas Young finally getting a chance to show his dream house to President Washington.

In 1905, millionaire Bernard Baruch bought Hobcaw Barony, which included Bellefield Plantation. He gave the former plantation to his daughter Belle. The young heiress had taken flying lessons and then bought her own plane, which she often flew over Bellefield Plantation, intrigued by the nature and wildlife she saw. In addition to being a pilot, Belle was a skilled yachtswoman and an accomplished equestrian who won hundreds of titles worldwide. In 1936 she decided to build a house and stable on the property. Belle had found the deteriorated house and noticed that it had the best view. She told the architects she felt a fondness for the old dwelling and asked them to find a way to incorporate it into the new construction.

Belle Baruch had heard the stories about the ghost of Thomas Young and decided that the original building and ghost story would add a certain charm to her new home. However, the architects informed her that there was no way they could make use of the rotting structure; unless she wanted to build her house elsewhere, they would have to remove the original building. So the old edifice was razed and a beautiful new home replaced it. The ghostly figures and mysterious bobbing light were never seen again.

A Presidential Visit

President Franklin D. Roosevelt visited the house in April 1944. War raged in Europe and the president had been under an inordinate amount of stress. His health was suffering—he had lost a good deal of weight, and was absolutely exhausted. He accepted a longstanding invitation to Bellefield Plantation and spent a full day in the quiet company of Belle Baruch. President Roosevelt relaxed in front of the fireplace, enjoying both the good food and the stories his hostess provided. The ghost of Thomas Young was among the entertaining tales Belle told her guest. Because of her superb hosting skills, Belle entertained many important people at Bellefield until her death in 1964.

She left Bellefield and Hobcaw Barony, along with 15,000 acres, to the state of North Carolina. Bellefield burned down many years ago, but Hobcaw Barony still exists and is open to the public during the week. There is a small museum on site. The former plantation is located 35 miles south of Myrtle Beach and just 2 miles north of Georgetown. Look for signs along Hwy. 17. For more information call 843-546-4623 or visit their web site at http://hobcawbarony.org.

They were afraid that others might think them crazy, so they never told anyone what they saw.

The Shoo-Fly was chugging along its route one night in 1906 when it crashed. The wreck occurred because an earlier train had accidentally tripped a switch. It seems there was a piece of lumber that stuck out of a freight car just far enough to clip the switch, leaving no track for the next train to follow!

When the Shoo-Fly came barreling down the railroad tracks between Warsaw and Wilmington, it jumped the tracks where the switch had redirected it. This resulted in the train doing a nosedive down the steep embankment. Loud, hysterical screams rang out as the passengers realized what was happening. It must have been an awful sight to see that iron horse careening to its doom.

The engineer, fireman, and conductor were killed when the train wrecked. Remarkably, all the passengers lived (although it is doubtful they ever boarded another train). The Shoo-Fly's engineer, Gilbert Horne, was the father of the earlier train's engineer, Will Horne—imagine how poor Will must have felt, upon realizing that neither he nor anyone else aboard his train noticed their fatal mistake with the switch!

Until recently, many different folks witnessed the train's "choo choo" horn and bright lights. Some lived in the vicinity, while some traveled quite a distance just to see the legend for themselves. Some were young, while others were quite old. Some couldn't believe what they had seen. They were afraid that others might think them crazy, so they never told anyone what they saw. Others told everyone who would listen that they had seen the legendary Shoo-Fly Train. The ghostly train has been seen and heard during the day as well as at night. The sightings have all occurred in the Warsaw, North Carolina, area.

To see for yourself, take I-40 to the Warsaw exit (Highway 24). Follow the road into town and then turn right on Highway 117 South. When you see the tracks, follow them to the outskirts of town. Approximately 2 miles later you'll see the switch that derailed the Shoo-Fly. The train has appeared as far away as the bridge, which is about half a mile from the infamous switch. Some believe the engineer, fireman, and conductor are still trying to complete their route to Wilmington.

Warsaw

Originally known as Mooresville and later changed to Duplin Depot, the community of Warsaw, North Carolina, was settled circa 1825. The name was changed in 1855 because of a beloved resident. The community remains small, with a perimeter of only 2.9 miles and a population of less than five thousand. It is about an hour southeast of Raleigh and an hour northwest of Wilmington. For more information, visit their web site at www.townofwarsawnc.com.

PIRATE SPECTER

He kicked the crumpled body into the hole and covered both bodies and all the chests with piles of sandy soil.

*T*he Civil War was coming to Charleston. All the islands around the port town were critical to this battle, and both sides knew it. Soldiers jockeyed to set up garrisons on them, especially Morris Island, Sullivan's Island, and Folly Island. Of course, some of these islands were inhabited, and the residents had to be removed for their own safety.

The 62nd Ohio Regiment was responsible for establishing a stronghold on Folly Island, so the Union commander sent some of his men to secure it. They were instructed to quickly and politely round up the residents, mainly free blacks, and put them on a boat to Port Royal. A young man named Lieutenant Yokum was one of the men assigned this duty.

It wasn't even noon, yet the island was already hot and humid, and Lieutenant Yokum was outfitted in full uniform. July in the Lowcountry was a miserable time of year, marked by oppressive head and swarms of insects. During the summer, most planters took their families to visit relatives or friends who lived elsewhere. The soldier just wanted to get this over with, but he had trouble at the first house he approached.

The shack looked like one good wind would blow it away. As he started to knock, an old woman emerged demanding to know what he needed with her. Yokum was taken aback by her brusqueness, but explained that she was being evacuated for her well-being. The woman shook her head as he completed his sentence. When Yokum reiterated that this was an order from the United States government, the woman acquiesced.

Giving her a few more minutes to get used to the idea, he sat on the dilapidated porch and soon the two were exchanging pleasantries. Talk turned to life on the Folly Island, and she seemed eager to reveal all she had witnessed while living there. The old woman had seen many things during her lifetime, including horrendous hurricanes, shipwrecks, and pirates—she'd even seen pirates burying their loot right on the beach! The soldier fairly shook with excitement as she told her story.

According to the old woman, two pirates lugged several chests off their vessel, hurrying as fast as they were able. Considering their struggle, she surmised that the trunks were very heavy. The buccaneers were supervised by another pirate, presumably their captain. He watched and paced as they dug a hole wide and deep enough to bury the chests.

Twice, he took out a looking glass and surveyed the horizon in front of the beach. The woman was a little girl at that time, and had been playing on the beach when the pirates disembarked. She hid behind a big tree and watched these activities with great curiosity, which turned into horror as the captain killed the men who had buried his treasure. Apparently, he didn't want another living soul to know this secret. First, he hit one of the pirates with a shovel, knocking him unconscious and into the hole. Then, before the other pirate could react, the captain pulled out a pistol and shot him. He kicked the crumpled body into the hold and covered both bodies and all the treasure chests with piles of sandy soil. Despite the legends, pirates rarely buried their treasure unless they feared they might soon be caught red-handed. Only then did they bury their ill-gotten gains, hoping to return soon to retrieve it.

The British had been pursuing the marauders and caught up to the pirate captain as he was setting sail. He was arrested and never did return for his buried treasure. Treasure seekers heard the rumors and came to the island to dig for buried treasure. The island had been dug up many times over, but if anyone got close to the actual spot, he was scared off by the sudden appearance of a sinister pirate specter.

Yokum had a little difficulty understanding some of her story because of her accent and dialect. But he was fairly certain he had managed to interpret it with reasonable accuracy until the end.

"You mean no one's ever found the treasure?" he asked in disbelief. The woman vehemently shook her head several times.

"You never tried to dig it up yourself?" he asked in amazement.

"Looord, no! Dat treasure is cursed. No good come of disturbing da dead, yanh. Evil . . ."

Yokum couldn't understand the last couple of sentences but he didn't care. He wasn't interested in a lecture. Buried treasure was a different story. As he was reflecting on her outrageous tale, he remembered his mission. The young lieutenant finally persuaded the old woman to leave. He helped her gather her few precious belongings and got her to the boat. By late afternoon, all the inhabitants had been taken off the island. That night, Yokum and his buddy, Lieutenant Hatcher, sneaked over to the place the old woman had indicated. Yokum had repeated the story to Hatcher during supper, along with the fact that he believed the woman was sincere. Hatcher had agreed they had to pursue the possibility.

They found the site without much difficulty and began to dig zealously. Within a few minutes, the sky flashed several times, just like lightning—only there was no storm. Next, a pirate specter appeared just a few feet from the men and began to reach for his holster. The soldiers looked at each other, then turned and ran back to camp. They never looked back.

Lieutenant Hatcher died in battle and Yokum never told anyone about his experience until many years had passed. Some of the men who served in the 62nd Ohio Regiment during the War Between the States reunited. During the reunion, Yokum shared his tale with Francis Moore. They were all old men by then and Yokum saw no harm in his reflection. Moore was so fascinated by the story that he wrote down everything Yokum told him. Rumor was that he wrote a book about it, but I was unable to find such a publication. It would be an out-of-print title, and such a rare book would probably have significant value.

I've also heard another version of this story, which I included as "Buried Treasure" in *Ghosts of the Carolina Coasts*. That version goes like this:

"Aye, what a glorious booty!" the pirate exclaimed. The buccaneer and his band of pirates had just successfully seized a Spanish galleon's cargo, including gold and silver, jeweled religious icons, silks and fine linens, muskets, and two kegs of gunpowder.

They landed at a stretch of beach near Charleston, to hide out and celebrate as only those who have endured life at sea can. As the merrymaking grew in intensity, one of the crew ran to the captain and told him he had spotted a military ship on the horizon.

Knowing this meant the U.S. Navy had found them and was on the way to capture them and recover the treasure, the captain had it hidden.

"If anyone tries to dig up my riches, they will have to get past me, alive or dead!" he threatened. And with that, the pirates got ready for battle.

The sea robbers fought the good fight, but were ill prepared for such a confrontation. They were outmanned and outmaneuvered.

The captain was killed, along with the rest of the small group of tired, drunken pirates. The crew of the navy vessel searched the island and the marauder's ship, but couldn't find the loot. They spent several days excavating the surrounding tract of coastal ground, but short of digging up the entire island, determined it would be impossible to find the hiding spot. The officers finally gave up and called off the search.

The story circulated that there was buried treasure at Charleston's Morrison Island, now known as Folly Beach, and that it belonged to anyone who could find it. Treasure hunters soon filled the island, shoveling up sand, dirt, bushes, and trees in hopes of finding a fortune. Not one of these men, women, or children came close to the burial spot.

After the initial frenzied efforts turned up nothing more than debris and junk, people began to believe that the pirate never buried any "booty" on Morrison Island. Attempts to discover the treasure became few and far between. However, a group of soldiers stationed at nearby Ft. Moultrie decided to try. As the men inadvertently came close to the treasure, they saw an immense man in pirate garb standing with his hands on his hips and a shimmering silver sword at his side. Before they could talk it over and figure out what to make of it, or what to do, one of the men advanced towards the figure. A freak earthquake, the only one of any consequence to hit the Charleston area, occurred at that moment and took the man's life. The others fled, terrified, believing the menacing-looking pirate had appeared to warn them to stay away. They swore they'd never set foot on the island again.

Others have tried to take the treasure, but they also claimed to see the dead buccaneer. They had heard the sight of him was a final warning, and they wisely took it as such and left.

Another group of determined men tried to find the fortune. As they came ashore, they noticed the darkening skies and the sea starting to get rough, but dismissed it as their greed for the gold outweighed their common sense. After a couple of hours, the men accidentally neared the spot. There stood a massive figure grasping a long, gleaming blade pointed in their direction.

Some of the men started back to the boat, while the others continued towards the figure. The foreboding pirate raised his cutlass as they closed in on him. The rest of the men suddenly turned on their heels and ran to the boat to catch up with the others, anxious to get away. Despite the high and extremely rough swells created by the violent storm that embraced the island, the men pushed the boat into the water and jumped in.

The first man to flee after witnessing the pirate was found the next day, clinging to the side of the boat. None of the other men were ever seen again. To this day, no one claims to have excavated the treasure that the dead pirate captain so closely guards.

FENWICK CASTLE:

When the girl looked from her bedroom window, she cried out in horror at the sight.

I am so happy. I never thought I could be so happy!" exclaimed Ann Fenwick.

"You make me far happier, sweetheart," Tony, her fiancé, said.

"Is it possible? To be happier, I mean?" Ann asked.

"Yes, and that is to greet each new day with you beside me," Tony replied.

At this comment, Ann's expression darkened. "My father will be furious!" Ann involuntarily shuddered at the thought. Lord John Edward Fenwick was not a man accustomed to trickery, and his daughter knew he would not take kindly to it. Still, there was some small comfort in the fact that she and Tony would be married by the time her father learned of the deception.

"Your father doesn't think I'm good enough for you, and I dare say that he is right. Still, he will have little choice in the matter if we are already wed by the time he learns of our relationship," said Tony.

She turned and looked adoringly up at his handsome face. He leaned down and kissed her. "We better get back before he sends someone looking for us," he said quietly.

With Tony's assistance, she mounted her horse and they rode in silence back to the stables. Could it only have been a few months since she met Tony? She pondered all that had happened. Lord Fenwick had hired a groom to take care of his stable full of horses, including a beautiful stallion he had sent all the way from England. It was rather indulgent, she mused, but oh, how she loved her horse. And it was no sillier to go all the way to England to get a fine horse than it was to build a castle on Johns Island just to remind you of the Fenwick family home in England.

She knew she should be grateful that her father was so particular or he wouldn't have fired the last groom and hired Tony. If he hadn't done this, they would surely never have met and fallen madly in love. She glanced over at him. He was much more mature than the young men she had met at social gatherings in Charleston and at area plantation parties. Of course he was several years older than she was, but there was nothing unusual about that. It was the fact that he was a groom that doomed him with her father.

"Never!" he roared when she once mentioned that Tony had expressed interest in her. "If I ever hear you mention such nonsense again, I will fire him and send you off to school in Charleston!" he threatened. She knew her father meant it, but she also knew she couldn't choose whom she loved.

It all started because Ann loved to go riding and her father forbade her to go alone. As a result, she and Tony spent many hours together riding the trails, picnicking, and talking. The more she learned about him, the more she liked him. He was fiercely independent and had some pretty ambitious plans, which she hoped would impress her father.

They turned into the stables and Tony helped her off the horse. "I'll see you tonight," he whispered as her piano teacher stood waiting to whisk her inside for her afternoon lesson.

Ann awoke in the wee hours of the morning, as planned. She reached for her small suitcase that she had carefully packed and placed under her bed before going to sleep. She dressed in travel clothes and slid noiselessly out of her room, pausing long enough to listen. She could hardly believe she was really about to elope. It didn't seem real even as she made her way down the secret staircase and into a small tunnel that led from the house to the Stono River. Her great uncle had been a pirate and he used to hide there from time to time, along with his ill-gotten goods. How grateful she was for the secret passageway tonight.

Tony was waiting in their usual secret meeting place. He had her horse saddled and ready. He took her small bag and carried it on his horse. They rode off towards Charleston just as daybreak arrived. Tony had already made all the arrangements during his day off, including arranging for the reverend's wife to serve as their witness. It wasn't the grand ceremony that Ann had always envisioned, but she had already accepted the fact that she and Tony couldn't have a big wedding.

Tony had hired a carriage and it was waiting outside for them. They held hands all the way to the honeymoon cottage he had also arranged. The couple shared a lovely meal and retired early. They awoke early in the morning and collected their belongings. The honeymoon was over. They had allowed themselves one night before they faced Lord Fenwick. Ann had left a note on her bed telling her family not to worry, that she was all right, and that she was with Tony. They both knew that Fenwick would not only send out search parties but that he would never forgive his daughter if she didn't quickly return to explain.

Tony had already secured another job as a groom at a nearby plantation. There was a small cottage on the property, which was where they had spent the night, with the owner's permission, and where they would begin their life together if Fenwick didn't accept the news well. Tony was sure he would immediately throw him off the property. They would wait at the cottage to see if he would finally accept the inevitable. Still, he hoped it would all blow over soon because he couldn't stand the thought of his bride being the hired help's wife and having to live in the groom's cottage.

He hoped Ann was right in thinking that her father would be furious but would eventually calm down. She assured him that her father would want her to be happy and would never force her to choose between him and her husband. Tony hoped she was right. She was young and naïve and had led a sheltered life, and she was also Lord Fenwick's only daughter. Seeing the anxious look on his wife's face as they turned onto the road leading into the plantation, he squeezed her hand and smiled fondly at her. "It will be all right, dear Ann," he promised.

Her father was standing in the doorway before they could exit the carriage. Hands on hips and eyes blazing, he called out, "Where in the devil have you two been?"

Tony calmly told the irate father than they had eloped. "We were married in Charleston yesterday. We spent our wedding night in a house on the outskirts of town," Tony replied.

This news did it. Lord Fenwick ordered Ann into the house. As she stammered and protested, he shoved her towards the door. "Go! I have some business with your new husband," he told his daughter.

A servant urged Ann inside as John and Tony headed towards the stable. Ann stood in her bedroom, hoping the lecture that her father was giving her husband wasn't too severe. When the girl looked from her bedroom window, she cried out in horror at the sight. Tony was sitting on her horse with a noose around his neck. At that moment, her father slapped the horse's hindquarters, sending it forward. Tony was suspended in mid-air. "Oh Lord, no!" she screamed as she ran downstairs, out of the house, and across the yard as quickly as possible. But it was too late. A slave was already removing the body. Tony's neck had snapped the instant the horse took off, immediately killing him.

Ann never got over the horrific death of her husband. She had frequent nightmares about seeing him hanged, and she never rode her horse again. Her father told her she would thank him one day, but she never did. After Ann Fenwick's death, footsteps and cries were often heard in the house. Was it Ann running to meet her beloved to elope? Or running to try to save him?

GREAT DISMAL

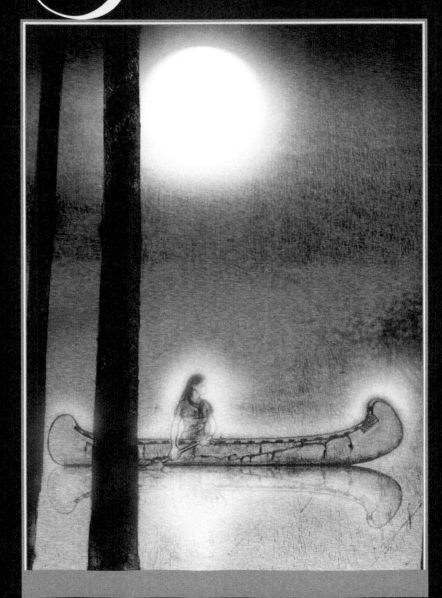

SWAMP SPECTER

So many people witnessed the strange sight that her grieving fiancé believed that she had risen from the dead and taken up residence in the swamp.

*H*e loved her so much that he could not imagine life without her. The day he proposed and she accepted was the happiest day of his life. He couldn't wait to begin his life with his beloved. There was no doubt that the Indian brave was as excited about the wedding as his bride-to-be.

Sadly, she died shortly before their wedding was to have taken place. The legend doesn't tell us what caused the Indian maiden's untimely death; it only says that a ghostly apparition resembling the girl has been seen paddling a canoe around Lake Drummond. The sight is all the more eerie because the canoe is bathed in a warm glow of surreal light.

So many people witnessed the strange sight that her grieving fiancé believed that she had risen from the dead and taken up residence in the swamp. According to Indian beliefs, a soul leaving a body and taking another form is entirely plausible. The bereaved youth abandoned his people and took to living in the swamp in the hope of joining his lost love.

No one knows what happened to the Indian brave, but the

Lady of the Lake, also known as the Great Dismal Swamp Ghost (or Specter), is still seen on occasion by fishermen and hunters. Over the years, some have tried to rationalize the sighting by claiming it must be moonshiners, pirates, outlaws, or foxfire (a luminescence originating from rotting wood or decomposing vegetation). The perfect combination of air, humidity, and flora and fauna could theoretically create an illumination of sorts, but if you ask me this theory seems less likely than ghosts!

"The Lake of the Dismal Swamp"
(poem based on legend)

But Oft, from the Indian hunter's camp
This lover and maid so true
Are seen at the hour of midnight damp
To cross the Lake by a fire-fly lamp,
And paddle their white canoe.

Thomas Moore, 1803

There's another swamp legend, this one about a deer tree. It is said that there is a huge, knotty bald cypress at Lake Drummond that was created by a deer. The animal turned itself into a tree to get away from hunters but was unable to change itself back. Another version is that a witch was out gathering ingredients for a potion when hunting dogs picked up her scent. The pack had her trapped at the edge of the lake, and in order to escape she chanted a spell that turned her into a tree. Unfortunately for the witch, she couldn't remember the spell to reverse what she had done.

Swamp History

The Great Dismal Swamp is a superb backdrop for all kinds of legends and lore. One of the reasons is that it is an extraordinary place. This ancient forest is home to many mammals, reptiles, and birds. There are nearly sixty species of turtles, frogs, and lizards and more than two hundred bird species. Once upon a time, the swamp was under the sea. A Continental Shelf shifted, causing the swamp to rise above sea level. In 1763, George Washington visited the swamp and proposed that it be dug out to create a canal that would connect the Albemarle Sound in North Carolina with the Chesapeake Bay in Virginia. Joined by several affluent North Carolinians and Virginians, he formed two companies: Dismal Swamp Land Company and Adventurers for Draining the Great Dismal Swamp. They spent $20,000 to buy 40,000 acres of swamp.

The plan was to drain the swamp, sell the trees for lumber and shipbuilding, and create good farmland. Needless to say, they soon realized the difficulty of their project. It was just too hard, too time consuming, and too expensive to drain and cultivate swampland. There is still a five-mile ditch that was named in honor of George Washington. Logging efforts continued until the land was donated to the Nature Conservancy. It became the Great Dismal Swamp National Wildlife Refuge in 1974.

The refuge, located in northeastern North Carolina and southeastern Virginia, extends into three counties: Gates, Pasquotank, and Camden. The protected area consists of

107,000 acres of wetland surrounding 3,100-acre Lake Drummond. Some people believe the tea-colored water has medicinal powers. The lake is named after North Carolina Governor William Drummond, who discovered the lake in 1665.

Great Dismal Swamp National Wildlife Refuge is located at 3100 Desert Road in Suffolk, Virginia. Visitors may enjoy a myriad of activities, including walking the one-mile Dismal Town Boardwalk Trail, hiking, biking, fishing (license required), birding, and photographing wildlife. Wildlife and nature enthusiasts will appreciate the diverse flora and fauna, such as the Typelo-bald Cypress, Atlantic White-cedar, Silky Camellia, Log Fern, red fox, otter, bobcat, black bear, and more than two hundred bird species. Small boats are permitted and there is a public boat launch just north of Feeder Ditch. Pay attention to signs indicating boating restrictions. Field trips and school programs can be arranged. For more information call 757-986-3705 or visit their web site at http://greatdismalswamp.fws.gov.

THE *CRISSIE WRIGHT* CAME ASHORE

Horrified, the Diamond City inhabitants watched as the ship floundered on the shoals, getting pounded by the huge waves.

"*A*ttend the main mast!"

"All hands to the rigging!"

"All hands starboard!"

Various commands were issued for the better part of an hour before the captain abandoned any hope of saving the ship.

"Launch the yawl boats!" Captain Jeb Collins ordered.

It was no use. The surf was so high and fierce that it was impossible to launch the lifeboats. Two men were nearly tossed into the rough surf trying. The captain was also experienced enough to realize that if, by some miracle, they could get at least one yawl boat into the water, it would never reach the shore.

"Abort!" he commanded, knowing that they would die that night.

When the wicked weather arrived, the captain had made the prudent decision not to attempt Diamond Shoals. He changed course to Cape Lookout Bight to avoid the treacherous shoals that even the most adept sea captains wished to avoid, even in good weather—during a terrible storm such as this, it would be suicide to attempt it.

A "worst case" scenario happened next—the main mast brace split. Without the mast, the sails and rigging had nothing to support them. There was nothing the crew could do.

"Drop anchor!" the captain ordered.

Both anchors were cast into the murky water, in the hope that they would keep the ship in the vicinity. The anchors couldn't do much in the rough sea. The vessel drifted onto the perilous shoals and was stranded. Every pounding wave delivered a beating to the ship. It would only be hours before the Crissie Wright washed ashore as shipwreck debris.

Diamond City was a whaling and fishing community that was located on the eastern end of Shackleford Banks. The horrified inhabitants watched as the ship floundered on the shoals, getting pounded by the huge waves. Some of the whalers tried to launch a rescue mission, but they had no better luck than the *Crissie Wright* crew had with their lifeboats. The surf nearly drowned the men before they could all get into the boats. One boat even flipped over and narrowly missed hitting a man on the head. Another man suffered a leg injury and had to be helped back to shore.

While the younger men kept trying to get their boats into the water, the older men gathered wood and made a huge fire. The women gathered blankets and made coffee and soup to warm whoever made it to shore. The ship looked like it was getting ready to break apart at any moment. The Diamond City residents hoped some of the men might be able to swim to shore. If they could make it far enough, the strongest swimmers might be able to bring them the rest of the way. It was a long shot and they all knew it, but they also knew the alternative.

And then it happened. A gigantic wave swept the captain and two crew members overboard. They were never seen again; they probably drowned almost immediately. As the night lagged on, the temperature dropped drastically until it was bitterly cold. Most residents were driven back indoors so they wouldn't freeze to death. All they could do was pray for the men aboard the sinking ship.

This is where the expression "cold as the night the *Crissie Wright* came ashore" originated. Long-time Beaufort, North Carolina, area inhabitants and descendents still use that phrase on terribly cold nights.

The next day dawned cold and the sea was slightly calmer. Some of the men set out for the *Crissie Wright* in the sturdiest whaling boat. Miraculously, they made it. When they got to the vessel, which lay on its broadside, they were met with a tragic sight. Only four men remained on board. They were wrapped in a sail and all had frozen to death except the ship's cook. He was a very large man and the extra fat probably helped insulate him from the cold. However, the long night took a huge toll on the man. He received excellent medical care at Charleston's Naval Hospital, but he never fully recovered, mentally or physically; he died less than a year after the night the *Crissie Wright* came ashore. The journey had begun in October 1885 in Rio de Janeiro and ended on January 11, 1886.

Claimed by the Sea

To the men of the *Crissie Wright* who gave their all but were claimed by the sea:

Captain Jeb Collins
First Mate John Blackman
Second Mate Sam Grover
Able Seaman Dozier
James Boswell, carpenter
Chester Simmons, cabin boy
Robert "Cookie" Johnson, cook

Only three bodies were recovered. The other men were lost to the sea. The three bodies were buried in an unmarked grave in the Old Burying Ground in Beaufort, North Carolina.

Some good came from the tragedy: more lifesaving stations were authorized along the Carolina coast. The Old Burying Ground is well worth a visit if you're in the Beaufort area. Maps detailing historic sites, including the cemetery (and common grave of the *Crissie Wright* crew), can be obtained at no charge at the visitor's center. As you will discover, the northwest part of the cemetery is the oldest, dating back to the early 1700s. By 1903, Diamond City was a ghost town—hurricanes had forced its inhabitants to move inland.

Excavation

The excavation of a wreck believed to be the *Crissie Wright* was begun during the summer of 2004. Sophisticated equipment, expertise, and technology helped the excavating company arrive at their conclusion. Some photos and additional information can be found on their website at www.computer-therapy.com/sidco/ghost.htm.

For more information on lifesaving stations, Shackleford Banks, and much more, go to www.downeasttour.com.

The girl ran all the way home and breathlessly told her family what had taken place.

I am aware of at least three different legends that deal with the origin of the Gray Man of Pawleys Island, South Carolina. The common element among them is that anyone who sees the Gray Man will not be harmed by hurricanes—legend has it that he appears just before a bad hurricane to warn Pawleys Island residents of the coming storm.

The first story is one of the most widely circulated, and for that reason I included it in *Ghosts of the Carolina Coasts*. It is a heartbreaking story about a young man who accompanied his sick mother to get medical treatments that were not available locally. He was gone for an extended period of time. When he returned, he asked his beloved to marry him and she said yes. On the way to the wedding, he encountered terrible weather and his carriage overturned. The young man was thrown from the buggy and killed instantly.

After his death the young man's ghost was seen by his fiancée when she was walking the beach. He warned her that danger was coming, advised her to leave, and then disappeared. Understandably, she was spooked! The girl ran all the way home and breathlessly told her family what had taken place. They packed and left that afternoon for their inland home. That night a horrific hurricane annihilated much of Georgetown County, including Pawleys Island. The house of the young woman was untouched.

The Gray Man might also be the ghost of Plowden Charles Jeannerette Weston. This legend revolves around two lovebirds: Plowden Weston and Emily Frances Esdaile. They met while Plowden was studying in England, and they fell in love. He returned to Georgetown to share his news with his family. His father handled the news of their impending nuptials better than Plowden had hoped—despite sending his son to England to receive a first rate education, he intensely disliked the British and their role in the emerging America. He believed the British aristocracy had far too much power given to them simply because they were titled; he also disagreed with the practice of giving aristocrats prime land in the New World just because they happened to be in the King's good graces.

Despite the opposing political views, the wedding went off without a hitch on a fine August afternoon in 1847. Because both families were wealthy, the couple received many outstanding wedding gifts, including Hagley Plantation. Their beautiful new home and all the surrounding land was situated on the Waccamaw River near Pawleys Island, where Plowden and Emily built a summer house. The lovely custom-built home still stands today; it is now the Pelican Inn.

The Westons led a blissful existence for many years, dividing their time between their fine plantation home and their lovely beach house. Plowden was known to be a kind and generous man. He helped out neighbors whenever he could. He offered his assistance without them even having to ask. When his slaves needed a place to worship, he built them one of the nicest chapels in all of Georgetown County. The couple was well respected and had many good friends. Their life seemed idyllic.

Their utopia was disturbed when the Civil War broke out.

Plowden Weston, a tried and true Confederate, led the Georgetown Rifle Guard, Company A, Tenth Regiment. The middle-aged man didn't have to serve, but he wanted to help any way he could. Weston warned the area residents when enemy troops were in the area or on the way and led risky assaults so that his neighbors remained safe. To his credit, he was courageous and conscientious. Even though he contracted tuberculosis during the war and was in poor health for a good part of it, he would not forsake his people. Near the end of the war, Weston was offered the job of Lieutenant Governor of South Carolina. He accepted the position so he could have the opportunity to make an even greater difference. He never had the chance, however, because his illness left him bedridden much sooner than anticipated.

He was buried at All Saints Waccamaw Episcopal Church, where he had been married years before. Some people believe the Gray Man is the spirit of Plowden Weston because he loved Pawleys Island and was one of its earliest inhabitants. Furthermore, he always did whatever he could to help his friends and neighbors. Perhaps he is still watching out for the people of Pawleys Island and coming to their aid with warnings about severe storms.

One of the former owners of the Pelican Inn, Eileen Weaver, believes the Gray Man is someone else—Mr. Mazyck, a former owner of the property. Mazyck inherited the property from his cousin Emily Weston. Emily was the widow of Plowden Weston. This ghost appears wearing a gray nineteenth-century suit. A Georgetown historian showed Mrs. Weaver many nineteenth century photographs; among them were pictures of Mr. Mazyck and his wife.

Weaver identified not only Mr. Mazyck, but Mrs. Mazyck as well—apparently her spirit also haunts the inn. Mrs. Mazyck appears wearing a nineteenth-century checkered dress with delicate pearl buttons down the front. Weaver says the woman was spotted so often that guests sat in the parlor on summer nights waiting for her appearance. The lady usually did not disappoint her audience.

When she appeared, she floated into the hallway and walked up the stairs. Mr. Mazyck has been seen far less often than his wife, and he only appears prior to severe storms.

One of the most historical structures on Pawleys Islands is the reportedly haunted Pelican Inn, which was built in 1858.

Elegantly Shabby

Pawleys Island is 4 miles long and one-quarter mile wide. It is on the Atlantic Ocean and is part of Georgetown County. The island forms the eastern tip of the Waccamaw Neck, which is a narrow peninsula that extends from Murrells Inlet to Winyah Bay, which lies between the Waccamaw River and the Atlantic Ocean. Residents describe their beach community as "elegantly shabby." The island is one of the oldest beach resorts on the Eastern seaboard, first used as such in the 1700s.

In the 1920s, the island was known for its house parties, a tradition that continued into the 1930s and '40s. College students from all over the state and beyond flocked to Pawleys during Easter break.

Some mammoth hurricanes have hit the island, including one unnamed storm in 1893, Hurricane Hazel in 1954, and Hurricane Hugo in 1988. Remarkably, only a few houses have suffered any significant damage, which is a testament to how indestructible the cypress buildings are. Or should we credit the Gray Man for warning the inhabitants so that they can properly prepare for the storms?

BROWN LADY

The ghost has been nicknamed "The Brown Lady" because she is seen wearing a plain brown dress.

This is a classic love story, but unfortunately not one in which the couple lives happily ever after. The young man had to go fight in the Civil War before he could wed his sweetheart, and he was killed in battle. After the family was told of his death, the boy's father broke the news as gently as possible to the young woman, who took the news worse than anyone had expected. She pined for her lost love. Family and friends left her alone—they understood she needed to grieve if she was ever going to get over her loss. They brought her tea and sat with her—when she didn't insist on being alone—and they accepted it when she declined invitations to dinner parties or dances.

After a while her friends and family became very worried. As more time passed, she became more withdrawn and depressed. She continued to wear her mourning outfit, which was an unadorned brown dress. Despite everyone's efforts, the girl could not be persuaded to get on with her life. She started taking long, solitary walks and was sometimes gone for hours. More worrisome was the fact that she was barely sleeping or eating. Sadly, the distraught girl died less than a year after her fiancé. While this was clearly due to forgoing food and sleep for months, the cause of that was a broken heart. She had, quite simply, been unable to accept her true love's death.

She has been seen on the Chowan College campus ever since her death. Because she had been a student when she became engaged, many theorize that her spirit returned to a happier time when the future held great hope and joy. The ghost has been nicknamed "The Brown Lady" because she has been seen wearing a plain brown dress. The greatest chance of seeing her is near the Columns Building, although no one is sure exactly when she was last seen. Some folks I talked to said she was seen "just a few years ago" and others were even more vague with answers like "I don't know" or "Seems like someone told me about a sighting the other year."

During the 1940s and 1950s, the college used to hold annual Brown Lady Festivals. Votes were cast for the perfect "Brown Lady," and the winner wore a brown dress and became an honorary "Brown Lady." The festival culminated with a visit to the Wise Cemetery, which was close to the college. The idea was to remind students of the long-standing history, traditions, and ideals of Chowan College.

Murfreesboro

Chowan College is located in Murfreesboro (Hertford County), North Carolina, between the Roanoke and Chowan Rivers. Murfreesboro is part of the Albemarle area, which is in the northeastern part of the state. It is roughly one hour from Norfolk, Virginia, and two hours from Raleigh, North Carolina. You can reach Chowan College at 200 Jones Drive, Murfreesboro, NC 27855, by calling 252-398-6500 or 800-488-4101, or through their web site, www.chowan.edu.

Before this area was settled in the late sixteenth and early seventeenth centuries, its inhabitants were mostly Indians, including the Chowanokes, Meherrins, and Nottoways. Murfreesboro was also the boyhood home of Dr. Walter Reed, who made a monumental contribution to medical science when he discovered the cure for yellow fever. There are many lovely homes in Murfreesboro's Historic District, which you may admire independently or on a tour. Visitors will appreciate the Wheeler House, Blacksmith's Shop, Winborne Law Office/Country Store, Hertford Academy/Southal Cemetery, Rea Museum, and Brady C. Jefcoat Museum. Stop in at the Roberts-Vaughan Village Center for more information.

GHOST OF

She was closing up for the night when a barstool levitated off the ground and sailed across the room.

Zoe St. Amand lived at 72 Queen Street with her sister, Liz St. Amand, for most of her adult life; the sisters shared the bottom of the house. Their mother had died when Zoe was just six years old. She was a shy child and grew up to be an introverted adult. Zoe was the stereotypical spinster, and a dedicated teacher at the Craft's House School, which was just up the street on the corner of Queen and Legare Streets. She led a quiet life until her death in 1954.

Zoe's former residence, which was built in 1886, is now a popular restaurant called Poogan's Porch. Before it became a restaurant in the 1970s, the building served as a storage space for the Mills House Hotel, which is located across the street. Zoe makes regular appearances at the restaurant; she makes her presence known not only by showing herself to employees and patrons, but also by opening doors, tripping the alarm, scaring the dog, and brushing up against patrons and employees. She also causes disembodied paranormal phenomena, including moving objects throughout the kitchen area and knocking pictures off the walls. Although she is a mischievous ghost, Zoe has never been known to cause harm. She usually appears as an older woman in a long black dress with her hair worn in a tight bun.

It's believed that Zoe returns to 72 Queen Street seeking attention and love, the things she died without. She died alone—she had never married and outlived her beloved sister, Liz, by nine years. Now her spirit thrives on the constant respect and attention doled out by those who tell of their experiences with the ghost on Queen Street.

When Bobbie and Chuck Ball bought the house in 1976, a loveable little pooch, Poogan, came with it—the previous owners had moved and left him behind. He sat on the porch greeting patrons and visitors until his death in 1979. This is, obviously, how Poogan's Porch got its name.

When Chuck's stepfather Keith Tracy was working on some renovations to the restaurant, he heard loud banging coming from the bar area and went to see who it was, thinking it must be his stepson. No one was there. Dismissing the noise, he paused to sip the full cup of coffee he'd left on the bar a few minutes ago, but the cup was half-empty and there were lipstick marks on the mug. Another eerie occurrence made Bobbie Ball a believer in December 1999. She was closing up for the night when a barstool levitated off the ground and sailed across the room. The spirit has also brushed up against Chef Isaac Vanderhorst on a couple of occasions.

Stop in to sample some of their delicious Lowcountry cuisine, and perhaps you too will encounter the spirit of Zoe St. Amand. At the very least, you'll have an enjoyable dining experience and a chance to hear what Zoe has been up to recently. Poogan's Porch is located at 72 Queen Street, Charleston, SC; for more information call 843-577-2337 or visit their web site at www.poogansporch. com.

Full of Ghosts

 This city is arguably home to more ghosts than any other locale in South Carolina—it's even said that you can't spit in Charleston without hitting a ghost. If you'd like to learn more about Charleston ghosts, you can check out my earlier books, *Ghosts of the Carolina Coasts* and *The Best Ghost Tales of South Carolina*. Or simply enjoy one of the numerous ghost walks offered. Other opportunities for glimpses of ghosts include historic walking tours, pirate walks, bicycle tours, bus tours, carriage rides, harbor excursions, and more. For more information, contact the Charleston Area Convention & Visitors Bureau at 800-868-8118 or 843-853-8000, or visit their web site at www.charlestoncvb.com.

SPIRIT OF

More than a month later, a letter was sent to the family. It included a diagram with a large "X" denoting where a body was buried.

*I*n 1898 Mr. and Mrs. Cropsey moved into Seven Pines, a lovely home on the Pasquotank River. Cropsey, who had been a northern businessman, came to Elizabeth City, North Carolina, to try his hand at farming. In the late 1800s, many Yankees like him came south to take advantage of the real estate market. The plantations had suffered damage during the Civil War, and the necessary repairs were sometimes extensive and unaffordable. Because of this, many Southerners who had fallen on hard times were forced to sell homes that had been in their families for generations.

The Cropseys had several sons and daughters. Nell Cropsey and her sisters were all attractive girls. Nellie was stunningly beautiful, and it is said that she could have had her pick of suitors. Unfortunately, if two juries are to be believed, she chose poorly.

Nellie fell for a young man named Jim Wilcox. They had begun spending time together soon after the Cropseys moved to Elizabeth City. It quickly turned serious and Nellie dated Jim exclusively. After nearly three years, her patience had expired. The twenty-five-year–old man still had not proposed marriage. Nellie, who was getting to be an old maid at the age of twenty, threatened to end the relationship if he did not propose very soon. She taunted him by telling him of other suitors who would be thrilled to learn that she was free to see whomever she chose. Their discussion got so heated that her father came into the sitting room to make sure everything was all right. Nellie ran up to her room and Jim stormed out of the house.

Nellie Cropsey was never seen again. A popular theory is that Jim came back later that night and threw pebbles at her window until Nellie opened it. He may have tricked her into sneaking out to meet him, and may even have apologized for the argument. But if the bachelor didn't propose, Nellie probably would have broken up with him. He could have murdered her in a rage, and then buried the body.

Jim was a prime suspect in Nellie's disappearance, but without a body no one could prove that a murder had occurred. Residents searched for days but still no body was discovered.

More than a month later, a letter was sent to the family. It included a diagram with a large "X" showing where a body was buried. For some reason, this note was ignored. Five days later, a corpse was found just where the note said it would be. It is not known what finally made the family and local authorities follow up on the letter, or why it was dismissed in the first place.

When the authorities confirmed that the corpse was Nellie's, and that she had indeed been murdered, the logical suspect was arrested. Jim Wilcox was tried in 1902 and found guilty of first-degree murder. He was to be hanged for the heinous crime, but the North Carolina Supreme Court overturned the verdict. The court didn't think Wilcox had gotten a fair trial. In 1903, he was retried in Perquimans County rather than Pasquotank County, where the original trial had taken place. Everyone in Pasquotank County thought he was guilty, so his best chance of a fair trial would be elsewhere. He was found guilty of second-degree murder and sentenced to thirty years in prison.

In 1920, the governor pardoned him. He became a hermit for the next few years, and eventually committed suicide by shooting himself. Many believed he did it because his guilty conscience was eating away at him until he could stand it no more. It was widely believed that he sent the note showing where the body had been buried to ease his conscience and to ensure that Nellie got a proper burial.

The spirit of a beautiful young woman used to be seen roaming around the river, near the spot where Nellie's body was found. A few claim to have seen her at her former home on Riverside Avenue. It seems Nell Cropsey did not accept her terrible fate, or perhaps she is trying to help us uncover the truth.

What if Jim Wilcox wasn't the murderer? Nell's older sister, Ollie, had a suitor named Ray Crawford at the house on the same night Nell vanished; he may have had a crush on Nellie. He could have heard Nellie and Jim's argument and taken advantage of the situation. What if Ray came back that night and got Nellie to come outside and meet him? What if he told her that Jim wasn't good enough for her, and that he was never going to marry her? What if he laid out his true feelings for her and she told him to forget it, or worse, laughed at him?

The above scenario could have happened. Shortly after Nellie's murder, Ollie broke it off with the young man, and no explanation as to why she abruptly stopped seeing Crawford was given. After Ollie stopped seeing Crawford, she became a recluse. The theory that Crawford was the real murderer would explain why Ollie had shut herself off from the world. She might have suspected Ray and blamed herself for what happened. Crawford himself later committed suicide, but the reason was never discovered.

Nell's brother, Will, also killed himself in 1913 by swallowing poison. No explanation for his suicide was ever discovered. What that has to do with the whole sordid affair, if anything, is anybody's guess.

Jim Wilcox was pardoned in 1918. A few years later, he made a deal with a newspaper editor to write a "tell-all" book, but Jim backed out of the deal before work on the book began. Later, the reclusive ex-convict asked the newspaper editor to come see him. Jim killed himself a few days after this clandestine meeting. No one knows what was revealed during that private conversation, or why the editor never pursued the project after Jim's death. Maybe he promised Wilcox he wouldn't write the book, or perhaps he felt it was in bad taste to dredge it all up after the suicide.

With three suicides and a murder, it's a wonder there is only one ghost in this story.

Elizabeth City

Elizabeth City, North Carolina, is perched on the banks of the Pasquotank River, whose name means "where the currents divide." The waterfront town, which was founded in 1793, is the headquarters of the biggest Coast Guard rescue and training facilities in the United States. Its importance grew when the Dismal Swamp Canal was finished in 1805. The canal affords easy transportation of goods to Virginia, especially Norfolk. The area's history is showcased in the Museum of Albemarle in Elizabeth City. The city has five historic districts, and it has been featured in Norm Cramton's *The 100 Best Small Towns in America*. Boaters are especially fond of the area because of the Pasquotank River, Albemarle Sound, and the Intracoastal Waterway. For more information, see www.elizcity.com.

If you'd like more details about this fascinating legend, check out Bland Simpson's *The Mystery of Beautiful Nell Cropsey* (1993).

HATTERAS JACK

The dolphin jumped, rolled over, and walked on its tail!

*T*he waters around Hatteras Inlet and along the Outer Banks have claimed thousands of seamen. Some of the bodies washed ashore, which is how Bodie Island Lighthouse (once known as Bodys or Bodies Lighthouse) got its name. Others were washed out to sea, never to receive a proper burial.

Five things have kept the numbers of lost souls from being even higher: technological advances in navigational aids, lifesaving crews, lighthouse keepers, pure luck, and Hatteras Jack.

Who or what is Hatteras Jack? He is an albino bottlenose dolphin who delights in helping mariners. He used to appear whenever vessels entered Hatteras Inlet. Not only did the sea creature signal when it was safe to navigate the tide and traverse the channel, he even led the way.

In time, word about the special dolphin spread and captains began to look for Hatteras Jack, as he came to be called, as soon as they got to the area. If the dolphin didn't soon appear, they blew their foghorns just before they reached the inlet. Hatteras Jack always appeared and led them safely across the tricky inlet.

The best part was the show he put on after the journey was completed. The dolphin jumped, rolled over, and walked on its tail! It seems he knew he had done a good job and enjoyed showing off a bit.

Sadly, navigational aids improved so that Hatteras Jack was not needed as much as he once was. Eventually, the dolphin was no longer seen. Some believe he went somewhere he was needed more. After all, the world is full of hazardous shoals, inlets, and channels. Others feel the dolphin was the spirit of a seaman who was finally able to accept death once he was no longer needed to help his fellow seamen.

Hatteras Jack may feel his work is done, but nothing could be farther from the truth. This stretch of coastline is so treacherous that it has been nicknamed "The Graveyard of the Atlantic." More than six hundred ships have gone down along the Outer Banks. In 2003 Hurricane Isabel cut Hatteras Island in half, separating Hatteras Village, Hatteras-Ocracoke Ferry Terminal, and The Graveyard of the Atlantic Museum from the rest of Hatteras Island. The state spent more than six million dollars to fill in the large inlet that the hurricane created so that NC 12 could once again extend from Currituck all the way to the end of Hatteras Island.

He ordered his men to leave their bodies hanging over a little island situated deep in Hannah's Creek Swamp for the swamp creatures to dispose of.

*D*uring the Civil War it was unfortunately fairly common for looters to flock to a war-ravaged area. They hoped to steal any valuables that had been abandoned by residents or invading troops before they were able to return. In this case, a group called the Marauders came to plunder anything that the Union Army had had to leave behind when General Sherman's campaign went through.

The Marauders were scalawags from the north who were led by David Fanning. Their plan to plunder all they could lay their hands on ended when Confederate Colonel John Saunders and his men captured them. Normally the Marauders would have been taken into custody and eventually tried for their crimes. No way was that going to happen in this particular case. The Marauders had recently murdered Colonel Saunders' parents when they wouldn't surrender what precious possessions they had left. In retribution, Saunders hanged every last one of them.

He ordered his soldiers to leave the bodies of the Marauders hanging over a little island situated deep in Hannah's Creek

Swamp for the swamp creatures to dispose of—birds would poke out the eyes, and alligators, wolves, or possibly even wild boars would gnaw on the rotting bodies. Saunders thought it was a fitting end considering how they had "feasted" on the misery of others.

It is said that those who dare to venture that far into the dark, forbidding swamp will be subjected to the bone-chilling screams and cries of these tortured souls. What's more, they may witness the appalling sight of fifty ghosts drifting around this part of the swamp looking for peace, or possibly for forgiveness for the terrible deeds they committed while alive. Their punishment may be that they will never know peace in the afterlife.

Smithfield (Johnston County) is roughly 25 miles southeast of Raleigh on Highway 70. A campaign led by General Sherman's Right Wing and General Johnston's Army took place in March 1865; it included a big skirmish at Hannah's Creek. This resulted in a Union victory and 4,738 casualties. Three-fourths of the deaths were Confederate soldiers. General Johnston formally surrendered to General Sherman on April 26, 1865.

Just before she was hanged, the woman swore her leg and foot would appear on Buck's tombstone to show that she was kicking him from beyond the grave.

*T*his story begins in Maine with Colonel Buck, and ends in the Carolinas with his descendants. Colonel Buck was a successful businessman, prominent leader, and influential citizen of Bucksport, Maine. He founded the town, served as judge, and was a colonel in the Militia. He was also a devout Christian. As a deeply religious man, he had no tolerance for witchcraft. If there was even a hint of suspicious behavior, that was good enough for him to take action. Despite the fact that he was a judge, he required no proof that a person was a witch—hearsay was sufficient. (It is important to realize that this was the mid-1700s, not so long after the Salem Witch Trials of 1692. Folks were terrified of witchcraft and didn't always think logically.)

Ida Black was an old woman who lived on the outskirts of town and kept to herself. She appeared unkempt and always wore shabby black clothing. She was often seen mumbling, as if talking to herself or possibly casting a spell. That was all Buck had to hear. He had her charged with witchcraft and, despite the conflict of interest, he was the judge at her trial.

Ida Black was found guilty and sentenced to death. She didn't seem fully aware of what had happened until they were about to hang her. She could have been senile, which would explain her ramblings and poor hygiene. Ida begged the judge to spare her life, but his verdict was final. Just before she was hanged, the woman swore her leg and foot would appear on Buck's tombstone to show that she was kicking him from beyond the grave.

No one gave the threat another thought until Buck's death in 1795. An elaborate 15-foot tombstone was created in honor of the important man. The Buck Monument was the finest gravestone in the Bucksport Cemetery, but it secured itself a place in the history books and guidebooks for a different reason. Soon after the granite was placed in the cemetery, a shape appeared on it. Each day it became clearer, and within a couple of weeks it was obvious that it was a leg and foot

The family was deeply embarrassed and disturbed by the appearance of the shape. Furthermore, they didn't like the rumors going around that Ida had cursed Buck, and he was finally getting his just deserts in the afterlife. To end such ridiculous talk, they had the shape sanded off the granite, which was then polished to perfection. No one could tell there had ever been anything there, and the family was happy—at least until the strange shape appeared again. The family had the leg and foot shape removed several times over the years, but it always reappeared. No one even tries to remove it anymore. In fact, the monument is a tourist draw. It seems anyone who has heard the story just has to see if it is true.

This story came to the Carolinas when the Buck family migrated to South Carolina. They needed lumber for their successful shipbuilding business. Three towns were created because of the lumber mills: Bucksport, Bucksville, and Port Harrelson. The communities thrived, and Bucksville was more prosperous than Conway until the late 1800s. At that time the forests had been used up, and the workers moved on to other places. The schools and stores for the mill families were no longer necessary once they left these communities. The three towns were deserted and the Buck family lost their wealth. Many believed it was because of Buck's Curse—they said that Ida Black was no longer satisfied with only cursing Buck, so she ruined his descendants too.

The Buck Plantation (also known as the Road's End Plantation) still stands in Bucksville off Highway 48. Although it is in a state of disrepair, it remains on the National Register of Historic Places; the cemetery containing the gravesites of several of Colonel Buck's descendants is across the road. Bucksport is 11 miles from Conway in Horry County. The town covers only 3.8 square miles, and has roughly 1,000 residents. Port Harrelson no longer exists.

TALES OF THE

As he was plummeting to his death he let out a horrible scream.

*I*t's the Devil's work, I tell you," a young construction worker said.

"I definitely feel a chill every time I get close to the tower," a co-worker replied.

"Quit slacking off and get back to work," the foreman growled. "And don't be talking any more of such superstitious nonsense."

"It's not like we're making up stories. The tragedies speak for themselves," the first man replied. Most of the others nodded their heads in agreement.

It was hard to argue with them. They had lived in the Low-country their entire lives, and they had been raised to be respectful of signs. Some said that the first sign occurred when the Civil War broke out right after construction began on Prince Frederick's Episcopal Church. The building supplies made it all the way from England, but then the Union blockade kept the materials from reaching their final destination. The contractors had to go to a great deal of trouble to round up enough supplies to proceed with the project. This was no small feat, because everything was in short supply during the war.

If that wasn't a convincing enough sign that the Devil didn't want the church built, it was hard to ignore the next one. The project architect, Mr. Gunn, fell off the roof. As he was plummeting to his death he let out a horrible scream.

"I still hear his wailing when I try to fall asleep," a young man confided. "I just can't get it out of my head,"

"It was pretty horrible. No doubt about that," another man said.

Some of the men returned to work after the accident, but got so spooked when they got near the church that they immediately left. It didn't really matter since they couldn't obtain the necessary construction materials. The church, which was started in 1859, was not finished until 1877. The project was completed thanks to generous donations from other churches, as well as wealthy Northerners who had bought area plantations when their original owners fell on hard times. Although the building was still officially called Prince Frederick's Episcopal Church, it was commonly referred to as the Old Gunn Church ever since poor Gunn's death.

By the time construction on the church was finally finished, everyone had forgotten about Mr. Gunn's death, or had decided that it was just an accident. The church pews were full most Sundays, and folks were proud of their beautiful place of worship. It was also a gathering place for community events. Lovely robes were made for the choir by some of the ladies in the congregation. Because of the ornate robes and the fine church, the choir took special pride in their performance and often practiced from late afternoon until after dark.

Georgetown County suffered economically in the late 1800s. Rice and indigo production never returned to their antebellum glory, and many people had to sell their homes and move away. Since there weren't enough parishioners to pay for the pastor and church maintenance, the church closed its doors. It remained vacant for many years and fell into a state of disrepair. There was also a fire that did significant damage. The bell tower is all that is left of the grand old edifice, and there is a cemetery on the site.

Locals swear that sometimes at night the choir and organ can still be heard practicing. Some also claim to hear terrible cries when they have gone past the church ruins during the day—they say it's the voice of poor Mr. Gunn.

The church is southeast of Plantersville on Route 52. Take SC 22-4 (Plantersville Road), off Highway 701, sixteen miles north of Georgetown. It's a bit tricky to reach because of the water, so be sure to consult a map before setting out. Prince Frederick's Chapel Ruins has been on the National Register of Historic Places since 1974. There is a historic marker that reads "Prince Frederick's Chapel."

And the Sea

In March 1942, the Caribe Sea *sailed past Hatteras en route to Cuba. That was the last time his family saw Jim Gaskill.*

Nothing stays hidden in the ocean if she doesn't wish it to remain there. This tale is but one example of how the sea both gives and takes when she pleases.

Jim Baum Gaskill was born on July 2, 1916. His parents, Billy and Annie Gaskill, owned the Pamlico Inn on Ocracoke Island. Fishermen, seamen, and vacationers frequented the modest establishment. They did so not only because it was so clean, but also because of the hospitable nature of the proprietors. The Gaskills were charming hosts. The couple loved Ocracoke and couldn't imagine living anywhere else. They spent many leisurely Sunday afternoons out on the water exploring and fishing, and they passed their knowledge and passion for the sea onto their offspring, most especially to young Jim.

The lad grew up earning money on shrimp trawlers or fishing charters during school vacations. His parents also allowed Jim and his friends to take out the inn's dinghy, and they spent hours investigating the sound and inlet. By the time he was fourteen, Jim knew those waters like the back of his hand. While he loved Ocracoke, the youth yearned for greater responsibilities and challenges.

By the time World War I broke out, Jim Gaskill was a licensed captain. He joined the Merchant Marines and was assigned to take charge of the *Caribe Sea*, a freighter that helped keep supply lines open. However, she was not designed nor outfitted for combat—she was slow and equipped with only one gun. In March 1942, the *Caribe Sea* sailed past Hatteras en route to Cuba, and that was the last time his family saw Jim Gaskill.

Several days later, a terrible nor'easter came through the area. The Bankers were used to these storms and all agreed it was nothing out of the ordinary. Islanders hurried about picking up debris and making minor repairs. Bill Gaskill was checking the inn's dock for damage when he discovered a plank with the nameplate *Caribe Sea*. Even though the board must have traveled a long way, and even though there had been no official word from the government, Billy and Annie Gaskill knew the sea spoke the truth. Their son Jim was dead.

A few weeks later the United States War Department notified the family that Jim Baum Gaskill had died when the ship he had been serving on, the *Caribe Sea*, had been torpedoed by the Japanese. The island inhabitants trusted the sea so well that they had already held the memorial service.

A beautiful cross, crafted from the nameplate plank, can still be seen inside the United Methodist Church in Ocracoke Village. The inscription reads "In Memory of Capt. James B. Gaskill. July 2, 1916–March 11, 1942. This cross was constructed from salvage of the ship upon which Captain Gaskill lost his life."

And the sea will tell.

Millions of tourists visit Ocracoke Island every year. The island is accessible by private boat or public ferry service. *Photo courtesy of NC Tourism, Film, and Sports Development*

GHOSTLY

He yelled out to Fury, "Make me a winner or take me to hell!"

*B*ath is known for being one of North Carolina's oldest towns and a "City of Firsts." Bath had the state's first public library, port, shipyard, church, and resident pirate. It is believed that Blackbeard, the nefarious buccaneer, lived here briefly, and that during that time he was considered a local celebrity.

As far as legends go, this coastal community is best known for its ghostly hoofprints. It all began one Sunday during a traditional horse race. During a balmy October afternoon in 1813 or 1850, depending on which version of the tale you believe, young Jesse Elliot was tragically killed.

Jesse's ego and reputation were the culprits. He had won several horse races and with each victory his bragging got worse. "No one in the county can beat me and Fury," he declared. "I think Fury may be the fastest horse in the state!" Some folks got tired of his big talk and thought Jesse needed taking down a peg or two. Word spread that someone needed to beat him, but was there anybody out there who could beat this young man?

A fellow from a nearby town heard about Elliot from his cousin, and he was sure he could beat Jesse Elliot. Being a bit on the arrogant side himself, the young man told the townspeople that he was going to win the next race. Bets were placed between the citizens of both towns.

More people showed up for the race than ever before. The excitement was contagious. There wasn't much eating or visiting going on, which was unusual. Instead, race speculation and last-minute bets dominated the conversation. "I'll repair your wagon for free if Elliot doesn't win!" one man was heard to say. "We'll provide next Sunday's picnic supper if our boy doesn't come through!" another wagered. The women were just as bad. "Jesse sure looked nervous," one girl said. "He usually stops and chats for a few minutes before the race, but today he passed right by like I wasn't standing here!" "Nothing to worry about. Fury looks to be in fine form today, and he's the one doing all the work," another woman replied.

The conversations stopped abruptly when the command "Riders to your places!" was heard. The spectators fanned out along the road, jockeying for the best vantage points as the riders got into position. The white handkerchief was waved and the a "Go!" command accompanied its swift motion.

The five young men entered in that week's race took off simultaneously. Soon, however, the two youths who had both sworn they would win were in the lead. They were nearly even with each other. When one horse pulled ahead, the other soon surpassed him, and vice versa. As they neared the home stretch, Jesse saw that his competitor was a good head in front of him. He yelled out to Fury, "Make me a winner or take me to hell!" He kicked the animal's lower side belly a couple of times with the sides of his boots to make sure the horse went as fast as possible.

A strange and horrific thing happened shortly after Jesse's command to his horse. The animal stopped dead in his tracks, throwing the rider headlong into a huge pine tree. Jesse Elliot was killed instantly.

Sunday afternoon races were terminated for a long time after

Elliot's untimely death. Only a stump remains where the pine tree once stood. Before it was cut down, the tree had a remarkable appearance—one side was brown and dead, and the other was green and healthy. Because of this mysterious lopsidedness, there was no mistaking which tree was the cause of death.

However, something even more mysterious happened. Four unexplained hoofprints have appeared on the ground around that tree stump. Do they belong to Jesse's horse, Fury? Legend has it that anything that accidentally covers these tracks, such as leaves or sticks, or deliberately placed items, such as a cup or hat, will be found just outside of the hoofprints by the next morning. A former property owner who used to put out corn and grain to attract birds claims they wouldn't eat any that spilled into the hoofprints. The phenomenon was so well known that at one time a property owner charged an admission fee for folks to come witness the strange sight.

Nowadays the stump and mysterious hoofprints are on private property, and I have been told that the owner will have trespassers arrested. For your own sake, I will not divulge the exact location of the eerie hoofprints.

Bath

The town of Bath was founded in 1705, and is a National Register Historic District. If you visit, stop in the Bath Visitor Center, 252-923-3971 to pick up a self-guided walking map or find out about taking a guided tour and see a film explaining the town's history. Bath is on NC 92 or can be reached by Pamlico ferry. Visit www.nchistoricsites.org/bath

 ECRET SIGNAL

The young sailor sent a message to his love instructing her to put a light in the third-story window of the Heriot House once her parents were asleep for the night. This would be their signal that all was clear for him to come ashore to meet her.

A young lady was taking her dogs for their daily walk when she came upon a Yankee sailor. The young man was in town while his ship was unloading cargo and making preparations for their next voyage. In a busy port like Georgetown, this kind of activity was normal. The deep and instantaneous mutual attraction, however, was a first for both the young lady and the sailor. They began to meet every day when she took her dogs on their afternoon outing. The beautiful young girl hadn't had much experience with men because of her over-protective father. She found the clean-cut sailor to be attractive, funny, and knowledgeable.

The sailor entertained her by recounting his experiences and perceptions of places he had traveled while working on his uncle's ship. He enjoyed their time together immensely. She was a real lady, and he liked the way she seemed so interested in everything he said. He also liked her petite figure, porcelain skin, and long, silky blonde hair.

Who knows what would have happened if the girl's father

hadn't found out and intervened? Perhaps they would have married. Instead, he forbade his daughter from ever seeing the Yankee seaman again. He even went so far as to demand that the captain keep his nephew away from the girl or move his ship elsewhere. This put the captain in a difficult position—the girl's father was a prominent Georgetown businessman, and he certainly did not wish to anger him. On the other hand, he had never seen his nephew happier and was reluctant to meddle in another man's love life. So he did the only thing that made sense to him. The sea captain moved the vessel out of the dock and dropped anchor in the harbor, but made no suggestions regarding the romance to the young man.

The girl was devastated that her romance was over. But love prevailed and the young sailor sent a message to his love instructing her to put a light in the third-story window of the Heriot House once her parents were asleep for the night. This would be their signal that all was clear for him to come ashore to meet her.

With glee, the girl took the lamp upstairs and placed it on the sill of the dormer window. Then she cautiously made her way out of the house to their prearranged meeting place in the bushes next to the house. At that time the tall bushes were cut and arranged to be a maze rather than just a hedge, and there was a garden as well as a strolling area. The bushes were also great for privacy—a good thing, since the couple met in secret like this for nearly twenty years.

No one knows why the pair kept seeing each other without any apparent interest in furthering their relationship. Whenever his ship came in, she put the light in the window, and they had their late-night rendezvous. Then one day the sailor just didn't show up. The woman never knew if he lost interest or was lost at sea. She continued lighting the lamp, but he never returned. Eventually she stopped climbing the steps to put the light in the window—that is, until the height of the Civil War.

A Union blockade of Georgetown had cut off desperately needed supplies. The woman remembered how she used to place a light in the window so her beloved would know it was safe, and she start-ed using the same signal to let the Confederate blockade-runners know when they could safely come into the harbor. The woman may have lost her love, but she saved many lives during the war.

The Lady of Heriot House became a recluse, taking comfort mostly in the company of her canine friends. One day the dogs howled incessantly. When neighbors finally came over to investigate the reason, they found the woman dead, surrounded by her pets. There have been many owners of the Heriot House since that time, and they have described many inexplicable occurrences. A light is often seen under the door closest to the third floor room, although its origin has never been determined.

The light has also been seen outside the house, even though there hasn't been a lamp in the dormer window for many years. The last time was for Prohibition—the house was vacant during that time, so rumrunners put a light in the dormer window as a signal that it was safe to bring the contraband ashore. While it was unin-habited, the house deteriorated and took on a sinister appearance until it was renovated during the 1930s.

Perhaps even more disturbing than the mysterious light are the two supernatural figures that have been seen strolling in the side yard where the lovers used to meet. Or the sounds described as "dog toenails" that have been heard clicking across the hardwood floors of the old dwelling, even when no logical explanation can be given for the sound.

Georgetown

Heriot House, circa 1760, is now known as the Heriot-Tarbox House. It is a private residence located in Georgetown's Historic District at 15 Cannon Street. Georgetown is situated on the Atlantic Ocean where the Waccamaw, Black, Sampit, and Pee Dee Rivers meet to form Winyah Bay. The first land grant was issued in 1705. Free maps can be obtained at the Visitor's Center that afford an independent walking tour of the port city. Or you may opt to take an organized tour. All tours (except harbor excursions) depart from the front of the Rice Museum or on Front Street at the Visitor's Center. For more information, call 843-546-8437.

HAUNTED

Yelling commands to a couple of his men, he jumped over the side of his ship, shimmied down the ropes, and fell into the small boat attached to the ship.

*T*his extraordinary house, circa 1700, seems too serene for a place where so many deaths occurred. Nevertheless, its history is fraught with grim and gruesome events.

Let's start with Madison "Mad" Brothers, who killed another young man during a duel. The young captain was the epitome of a hard-nosed seaman, due in large part to the fact that he grew up on ships. The rough-edged man worked and fought for everything he had achieved. Brothers started out mopping the decks and doing other menial jobs, and he worked harder than any other crewmember. His ambition was both admirable and downright scary. He scrimped and saved and did a bit of conniving until he owned his own ship, which he captained himself.

Like many seamen, Captain Brothers often drank to excess. He was a nasty drunk whose temper often flared when he drank heavily. He provoked arguments and bullied his crew, but no one could complain. He was the captain and owner, after all. Rumor had it that he had even killed once in a fit of rage.

Socialite Samantha Ashby must have found his rugged demeanor appealing in a "bad boy" sort of way. The well-bred girl had almost assuredly never met anyone like him. He was a strong, good-looking man who had only shown her the best part of his personality. He fell deeply in love with the delicate, enchanting young woman, and Miss Ashby quickly fell in love with him. It was a whirlwind romance, and she soon agreed to be his wife, though if she had insisted on a longer courtship things might have ended differently.

At that time the Hammock House was an exclusive club for captains, and since Captain Brothers was a founding member, the couple decided to hold their wedding there. According to legend, every captain with routes along the eastern seaboard craved membership, and if one was admitted into the club, one had "arrived" and was thereafter respected by both seamen and society. The Hammock House got its name because it sat on a great hammock (knoll) at Beaufort harbor. The founding members gathered timber and fittings from around the world—the framework, stairs, doors, and porches were constructed of white oak, cypress, teakwood, mahogany, and rosewood, and the three-story dwelling was filled with impressive fireplaces and fixtures made of brass and copper.

Since Miss Ashby was from Baltimore, the wedding party had to travel to Beaufort, North Carolina. It was decided that she would come by stagecoach with her attendants and family friends. Sadly, she had been orphaned and the only family she had was a brother. He was a sailor and she had no way to reach him to invite him to the ceremony. Since they had always been close, she knew she should have waited until he was next in port so that he could give her away. However, Samantha had no idea when that would be and she was anxious to get married and go on the romantic honeymoon trip to the West Indies; she had never been there, but had heard amazing stories about the place from her fiancé and his fellow sea captains. So Samantha didn't mention her brother. Madison loved her so much that there was a chance he would want to wait until her only family could be a part of the nuptials. If they postponed the wedding, there was a chance he would have to put out to sea again, and then they would have to wait another year or two. Miss Ashby feared that he might meet another woman in some exotic port, so she was determined that the wedding must go on.

The bride and her entourage set out the same day that Captain Brothers and his crew set sail. The stagecoach arrived at Beaufort but there was no sign of Brothers' ship. Days went by and there was still no word. The bride might have been anxious if not for the pre-wedding festivities that kept her occupied. Grand bridal showers and teas were held in the afternoons, and small soirees began in the evening and went into the wee hours of the morning. Still, the young bride-to-be might have been sick with worry if she had not accidentally run into the one person that could make her forget all about her worries.

"Carr!" Samantha exclaimed from across a crowded room.

"Sam!" a familiar voice cried out.

A dashing young man scooped up the petite girl and spun her around in mid-air. "What are you doing here?" he asked in amazement.

"I'm here to get married!" she announced to her brother.

"No!" he countered. Looking around for a quiet place to talk, he was just about to suggest they step outside when a group of fellow officers approached. They quickly made plans to meet the next afternoon in the Old Burying Ground as Lieutenant Ashby was being hauled away to join his cohorts.

Meanwhile, Mad Brothers was mad as the Devil. His voyage to Beaufort had been disastrous and he was fed up. He'd had to turn around once and put into port with a very sick crewmember. The ship's rigging had gotten severely damaged during a violent storm, and a couple of days had been lost trying to repair it enough to finish the trip. New rigging would have to be purchased once he reached Beaufort. The weather had been foul and he hadn't loaded enough food for the extra four days. Unfortunately, Brothers had packed

135

plenty of booze and had taken to drinking rather than sleeping or eating.

Captain Brothers had just started to calm down when the ship finally turned into the inlet. He got out his spyglass and scoped out the Hammock House. Strolling around the grounds, arm in arm, was his fiancée and a tall gentleman in a naval uniform. That was the final straw! Yelling commands at a couple of his men, he jumped over the side of his ship, shimmied down the ropes, and fell into the small boat attached to the ship. The men followed, awkwardly climbing into the boat and lowering it down into the water. "Faster!" he commanded, as they rowed with all their strength.

At this point it was impossible to stop the events that had been set in motion. Mad Brothers stormed Hammock House, which the pair had already entered by the time he got to shore. Quickly scanning the crowd, he found Samantha and her escort dancing in a far too familiar embrace. Brothers pulled out his pistol, and then noticed that the man was armed only with a sword. Even with his temper, Brothers knew he couldn't just shoot the man in cold blood. He holstered his gun and unsheathed his sword, figuring he could just as easily kill him with that.

"Duel!" he challenged the rascal.

The officer looked shocked. He shook his head no, indicating he wouldn't fight him. Samantha looked horrified. "No!" she cried. Realizing what was about to happen, Ashby's friends stepped in and tried to stop the altercation. Brothers' men pointed their pistols at them, letting them know that this matter would only be settled between their boss and his adversary.

"You don't understand!" Samantha cried out as she grabbed at her fiancé and pushed her brother away.

Mistaking her tender act of affection as some sort of protective gesture towards her lover, Brothers went into a crazy rage. He charged the young man, again yelling, "Duel!"

Lieutenant Ashby had no choice but to fight or die. The air was quiet except for the sound of swords clashing and heavy breathing from the two men. Brothers was a superb swordsman and Ashby had been forced to retreat all the way up to the third floor—he was out of room and out of time. Taking a deep breath, he lunged forward and gave it his best. Ashby lost his footing and fell onto Brothers' sword. There may have been hope of survival had it not been for Ashby falling down the stairs with the sword in his chest. When he landed, the sword had buried itself deep into his body. He bled to death in just a few minutes.

Captain Brothers and his men beat a hasty retreat before retribution could be made. He never returned, and no one knows if he ever discovered that he killed Miss Ashby's brother, not her lover. Lt. Carruthers Ashby was buried in Beaufort's Old Burying Ground. Since Lieutenant Ashby was an officer on a British warship, HMS *Diligent*, he had made his wishes known should he die in battle. He had asked to be buried upright, standing at attention. There is a grave in the cemetery that is in such a position, but some say it belongs to another British officer who died in Beaufort. Without proof to the contrary, I'd say it's the grave of Lt. Carruthers Ashby.

To this day, faint bloodstains appear on the stairs to the third floor that cannot be eradicated. Sometimes, an orchestra, laughter, and clanking (like that of swords engaged in a deadly duel) can be heard. The Hammock House is the oldest house in Beaufort, North Carolina, and it is rumored that Blackbeard frequented it. At that time, the dwelling sat so close to Taylor's Creek that a boat could be tied up to its porch. This afforded a quick and easy getaway, just the way Blackbeard would have liked it.

Ghostly cries, both male and female, have been heard at the site. It is even rumored that Blackbeard hanged and buried one of his wives on the property. Some say it is her cries of protest that have been heard. Others swear the cries come from Samantha Ashby, protesting the fatal attack on her brother's life. Or perhaps they belong to poor Carr Ashby.

There may even be a different male ghost or perhaps a second spirit. It could be Richard Russell Jr. He allegedly took a slave up into the attic in 1747 to punish him for some improper behavior. The slave fought back and pushed Russell down the stairs. He broke his neck in the fall and died instantly. Some say it is his anguished cries that are heard.

As if all these tragedies weren't enough, another occurred on March 23, 1862. When the Union army seized control of Beaufort, three soldiers were sent to Hammock House. They were probably sent to make sure it was vacant and to check on its suitability as a headquarters or an officer's house. The three men were never seen again. In 1915, workmen accidentally found their bodies buried near the rear porch.

Photo courtesy of the North Carolina State Archives

Hammock House has served as a private residence, social club, inn, summer home, school, and accommodations for Union soldiers. It sat vacant for many years, which caused it to fall into disrepair. Thanks to the efforts of certain local citizens, renovations have been made to restore the lovely edifice. At one time, Taylor's Creek encroached right up to the front yard where there was a small dock. Today, the water is about 500 feet away. For more information, visit www.historicbeaufort.com/history.htm.

The Old Burying Ground

The Old Burying Ground, which dates back to 1731, is one of Beaufort's most fascinating sites. The cemetery was declared full in 1825, and the state government decreed that no more burials could occur here. It ordered Beaufort citizens to construct a new cemetery, but the residents kept right on burying their loved ones there until the early 1900s. Among the distinguished personalities buried in the cemetery are privateer Captains Josiah Pender and Otway Burns, as well as the crew of *Crissie Wright*, who froze to death when their ship sunk at Shackleford Banks. The Old Burying Ground is located in the 400 Block, Ann Street, Beaufort, North Carolina. For more information call 252-728-5225 or visit www.historic-beaufort.com.

PATRIOT GHOST

Many people have seen a large, shadowy shape outside the north window, and some claim to hear a man's voice calling outside that window, but when they look no one is there.

*D*uring the Revolutionary War, British troops seized Charleston (formerly Charles Town), South Carolina, in 1780. The British allowed Patriots to go home to safeguard their property, or so the agreement stipulated. In truth, many Patriots were held captive and their property, including their homes, heirlooms, and cash, was commandeered. As you can imagine, this made the Patriots all the more determined to distance America from British authority.

Colonel Isaac Hayne was an example of such a devout Patriot. The burly retired soldier was home taking care of his critically ill family when he was summoned to town to declare his loyalty. He must address whether he was a faithful and humble servant of the king or not. He could not stand the thought of falsely supporting the Crown he had grown to loathe, since the king did nothing more than tax and bully the colonists.

However, he knew if he did not sign the decree he would be imprisoned, and this he could not afford, even for a short period of time. Hayne had already lost one child to smallpox, and his other two children and wife were still battling the deadly disease.

He must return home so he could do whatever he could for them. Much as he abhorred the very thought, he must sign the paper. So that no one would mistake his reasoning, he wrote a lengthy letter to his good friend, Dr. David Ramsey, to reiterate that Colonel Isaac Hayne was, is, and shall always remain, a loyal Patriot.

His correspondence included this assurance, " . . . I will never bear arms against my countrymen. My masters can require no service of me but what is enjoined by the old militia law of the Province, which substitutes a fine in lieu of personal service. This I will pay for my protection. If my conduct should be censored by my countrymen, I beg that you will remember this conversation and bear witness for me that I do no mean to desert the cause of America . . ."

His two sons survived but his wife succumbed to the smallpox virus. Soon thereafter, the British sent orders that he was to join their army or go directly to jail. Instead, after a few clandestine meetings with some neighbors and townspeople, Colonel Hayne was granted a commission and joined the Patriots. He led an attack that ended in his capture. He was found guilty of treason and sentenced to death.

Custody of the two little boys had been given to their aunt, Mrs. Peronnau. Their father was permitted a brief farewell visit. Everyone was sobbing openly as Colonel Hayne was taken away by a British soldier. Many people had tried to help the colonel: notable citizens signed petitions; loyalists, who respected Hayne and thought the punishment was too severe, also interceded; even Lieutenant Governor Bull, who was quite sick and arrived by stretcher, appealed the execution. It was all to no avail—Lord Rawdon turned a deaf ear to all pleas. He wanted to make an example out of a Patriot leader, and nothing was going to change his mind.

Mrs. Perroneau kept the two boys inside her home on that fateful day. As the execution party paraded past her house, which was on the corner of Meeting and Atlantic Streets, she watched from a window. As he passed, Colonel Hayne yelled up to her that he would return. For many years after that, unexplained footsteps were heard coming up the exterior steps to the front door. The heavy steps sounded like they belonged to a burly man like Isaac Hayne. Many people have seen a large, shadowy shape outside the north window, and some claim to hear a man's voice calling outside that window, but when they look no one is there.

One man jerked the rider off the horse, and the other hit him hard in the back of the head with a heavy rock. He toppled to the ground like a sack of potatoes. The evil men dragged his body into the bushes to hide it.

*T*his story takes place in the early 1900s in the little town of Pactolus, near Greenville, North Carolina. A young man and woman were and engaged to be married. As he had done on several occasions, the youth rode his horse 6 miles from Greenville to Pactolus to meet his fiancée off the train. She was studying to be a teacher at East Carolina University; she had gone home to Virginia during the school break, and was returning on the afternoon train. The young man waited patiently, but the train never arrived. Realizing it must have been delayed, he decided he should head home. It was already dusk, and he didn't relish riding home in the dark. He hoped his horse could find its way.

Before he had gotten more than a few yards from the platform, a couple of men jumped out of the bushes alongside the railroad tracks. One man jerked the rider off the horse, and the other hit him hard in the back of the head with a heavy rock. He toppled to the ground like a sack of potatoes. The evil men dragged his body into the bushes to hide it. They took his watch and the little bit of money he had on him. They had planned to steal the horse, too, but it ran away as soon as the rider fell off its back.

The animal returned home a couple of days later. It looked worse for the wear and the family feared what had happened to the young man. After they tended to the horse, they sent out search parties—each pair of men followed a different route. The men looked everywhere but found no sign of the missing man. Sadly, one search party must have ridden right by the corpse on the way to the train platform. The body was eventually recovered and given a proper burial.

Ever since the young man was murdered, a strange light, commonly referred to as the Pactolus Light, has been seen near the tracks. It is believed that the murdered youth cannot accept his fate and still rides along the tracks awaiting the train carrying his beloved. Some claim the light is high up, like someone on horseback carrying a lantern, while others claim the light is low, like someone is on foot walking along the tracks. So many have seen the mysterious light that it is hard to dismiss it.

Rumor has it that looking for the light was a rite of passage and fraternity initiation for East Carolina University students until the tracks were taken up. I haven't found anyone who has seen the light since the tracks were removed. Since there is no way the train can pass through there anymore, it seems that the ghost has moved on.

However, if you want to try to see the ghostly light, there is a proper protocol. Follow the directions given below. When you get to where the field ends, flash your light three times. This lets the ghost know you are looking for him. If you are lucky enough to witness the light, do not try to follow it. The ghostly horse and rider believed to be responsible for the light will get spooked and take off quickly.

You will need a vehicle with four-wheel drive for this off-road adventure. Take Highway 264 East out of Greenville; go 6 miles east of the intersection of Highway 264 and Greenville Blvd. Here you will see a road sign for Pactolus. Approximately 1 mile ahead will be

Highway 30—turn left and follow the road for nearly 5 miles. Set your odometer and when it reaches 4 miles begin looking for Carl Morris, a dirt road on the left side of the highway. Turn left onto Carl Morris and continue for about half a mile. You should see a dirt trail that shows where the tracks were once laid. To the right is where the light will be, if it appears. Remember, be careful exploring ghostly sites during the day or night. You can get lost, harassed by locals or local authorities, or chased off private property (or worse!) if you are trespassing.

AUNTED

After the war, the hospital was no longer needed and the building was sold. Despite the low rent, no one wanted to move into the run-down building because of its terrible history.

Trapman Street Hospital was located at the corner of Charleston's Trapman Street and Trumbo's Court, off of Broad Street. It was a Negro hospital and later a hospital for Confederate soldiers during the Civil War. The long building was painted a bluish-gray and its columns were painted white. The facility had only eighteen rooms, plus a basement where the dead were temporarily housed.

During the war, every room was occupied by men in various stages of terminal illness. Some had lost too much blood from their injuries, while many others had infections that were slowly killing them—sanitation, both in the field and at the hospital, was a major problem. Painful wounds and a lack of pain relief brought anguished cries from the men throughout the day and night. As if their injuries weren't enough, the heat was intolerable, and the stench of death filled the air.

Charleston is in the heart of the South Carolina Lowcountry, where the high temperature and humidity are problems from late spring to late fall. The men were usually dehydrated despite the staff's best efforts. Most of them could not drink by themselves, which meant that someone had to carefully administer water to each patient. The water had to be drawn from the well by hand and carried up a long flight of steps. Ideally there would have been someone who did nothing but fetch water and give it to the men, but the hospital was short-handed so that was impossible. The staff did the best that they could, but there was little that could be done to keep the men comfortable.

After the war, the hospital was no longer needed and the building was sold. Minor renovations were made that turned it into cheap lodging. Despite the low rent, no one wanted to move into the run-down building because of its terrible history. A couple of prostitutes, a desperately poor woman and her daughter, Mary Simmons, eventually moved into the dwelling. They rented the rooms from landlord Henry Gardiner. These tenants, as well as neighbors living across the street, swore that strange things happened at the old hospital. Simmons said that when she was getting a bucket of water from the well, an invisible force took the bucket of water from her and carried it up the steps. The sound of heavy breathing and drinking followed. Then the empty bucket made its way back down the stairs and was given back to the girl! They also sometimes saw a shadowy figure wearing what appeared to be a soldier's uniform.

One resident, Daphne Trenholm, heard a commotion one night and left her room to investigate. She discovered a wounded youth lying on a stretcher and begging for water. She froze in fear and disbelief, but his repeated pleas finally propelled her into action. She grabbed a little half-full pitcher from her room, carefully made her way back downstairs, and gently held it up to his lips. He managed to lift his head a couple of inches. When he had finished quenching his thirst, the young man whispered, "Thank you" and let his head fall back onto the stretcher, his eyes closed. Trembling, Daphne ran back upstairs to her room. When she came out the next morning, there was no sign of the boy on the stretcher, but she knew she hadn't imagined him because her old pitcher was no longer cracked or stained—it looked brand-new!

The mysterious sounds disturbed the tenants and neighbors. Footsteps and cries could be heard when no humans were present. They knew it had to be the spirits of the soldiers who had been unable to accept their premature and painful deaths.

Mother Nature got rid of the run-down building. A storm severely damaged the roof, while an earthquake wreaked havoc on the foundation and chimneys. It was eventually razed, and for many years nothing would grow where the hospital once stood. Efforts to plant grass, trees, plants, and even the hardiest of shrubs came to nothing.

Trapman Street Hospital

Trapman Street Hospital was owned by Dr. Julian John Chisolm and managed by Dr. William Huger. Dr. Chisolm, a Charleston native, graduated form the Medical College of South Carolina. He wrote the Manual of Military Surgery (published in 1861), which became the official resource for treating Confederate soldiers. Dr. Chisolm invented the chloroform inhaler and was one of the first in the medical profession to use cocaine as an anesthetic. The patients were eventually relocated further inland, and that was the end of the Trapman Street Hospital.

Boo Hags

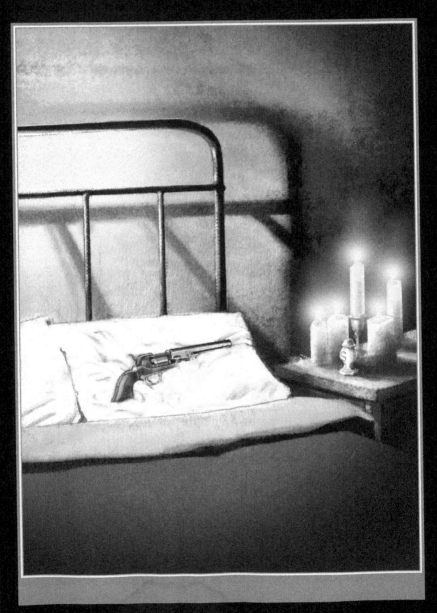

The scariest time to encounter a hag is at night, because when darkness falls she can shed her skin, rendering her invisible.

No book on coastal Carolina ghosts and legends would be complete without a discussion of hags, also called boo hags. According to the *American Heritage Dictionary* the hag is 1. An ugly, frightful old woman; a termagant; crone, 2. A witch; sorceress, or 3. A female demon.

In the South Carolina Lowcountry, we know so much about boo hags because of the Gullahs. Gullahs are descendents of West African slaves who worked on local rice plantations. After slavery ended, they remained on Georgia and South Carolina sea islands and in nearby communities such as Beaufort, Frogmore, St. Helena Island, and the Hilton Head area. They became fishermen, hunters, and farmers. They speak Gullah, which is an English-based creole that is marked by vocabulary and grammatical elements from various African languages.

Gullahs believe that people have both a soul and a spirit, and that upon death the soul leaves the body and returns to God, while the spirit stays on earth and participates in the lives of family, interceding whenever necessary. A boo hag is a bad spirit who uses witchcraft to persuade a person to do as she wishes. She can

How to Talk Gullah

Some Gullah terms:
B'leew = believe
Bukrah = white people
Cawpse = corpse, coffin
Dainjus = dangerous
'F'aid = afraid
Grabe = grave
Nebbuh = never
Ondeestunt = indecent
Pizen = poison
Skay'd = scared

even be hired to take care of a troublesome neighbor or rival love interest.

The scariest time to encounter a hag is at night, because when darkness falls she can shed her skin, rendering her invisible. She borrows a horse and uses it to transport her to her victim's residence. The next morning, the horse is usually found by his owner in bad shape, exhausted and with its tail full of knots.

If the hag is successful in gaining entry into the house, she sits on the victim's chest while he or she is sleeping. The person wakes up but is unable to call out for help or force the hag off his chest. The hag has been known to choke or suffocate her victims using this technique. There is no question it is the boo hag because the air is hot and moist and smells of rotting meat.

Fortunately there are some things you can do to confuse and elude the dreadful boo hag. One is to place a broom by the door—

hags will not pass a broom by day or by night. They are curious creatures and cannot resist the temptation to count every last straw on the broom. This is a laborious task and usually lasts until dawn. When the first light of the day appears in the sky, the hag is no longer powerful or invisible, so she must be gone by then. Other objects that confuse and torture the boo hag are brushes and sieves or strainers. They stop to count the bristles or the holes and lose most of the night in doing so.

It is said, though, that some hags have the gift of speedy counting. Because of this, other measures to confound them must be taken. For instance, painting the exterior doors and window frames indigo blue is said to ward off evil.

It is also believed that hags are afraid of gunpowder, so those fearing a visit from a boo hag should place a loaded gun under the pillow to keep evil spirits away. No one is sure why, just that this trick has worked successfully on many occasions.

The same holds true for lit candles. The smell of the burning candle keeps the hag at bay, so a true believer who has reason to suspect that he will be visited is likely to have his bedroom ablaze with candles. Furthermore, he will keep a salt shaker by his bed. If he smells rotting meat or hot, moist air, he will douse the air with salt. A salted hag is unable to get back into her skin, in which case she'll die.

Gullahs also believe strongly in prayers, curses, signs, and rituals. Some believe that a hag can be stopped if proper prayer incantations are applied.

One of the best places to learn about Gullahs and sea island history is the Penn Center & York W. Bailey Museum on St. Helena Island. The island is twelve miles from Beaufort. 843-838-2432 or www.penncenter.com. Penn Center Heritage Days Celebration is held every November and the Native Islander Gullah Celebration is held every February on Hilton Head Island. 877-650-0676 or 843-689-9314 or www.gullahcelebration.com.

There are a few companies specializing in Gullah tours, including Gullahtours.com. For more information, contact the local tourism agency.

Gullah Beliefs

• Never shake hands. It will put a curse on both persons.

• If a rooster crows at night, someone you know will die.

• Wishes made to a new moon will come true, as will dreams beneath a new quilt.

• If you see a red bird on your doorstep, count to nine and money will follow.

• Root doctors sell charms or mojo that can be chewed, worn, or buried, depending on the situation. The most common charms sought after are love charms, money charms, power charms, and health charms.

RESOURCES

North Carolina

North Carolina Division of Travel and Tourism
430 N. Salisbury Street
Raleigh, NC 27603
800-VISITNC or 919-733-8372.
http://www.visitnc.com.

North Carolina Ferry System
113 Arendell Street
Morehead City, NC 28557
800-293-3779 (800-BY-FERRY)
http://www.ncferry.org

North Carolina State Parks and Recreation Areas
Division of Parks and Recreation
Dept. of Environment and Natural Resources
P.O. Box 27687
Raleigh, NC 27611
919-733-PARK
http://www.ohwy.com/nc/n/ncparks.htm

A great tourism resource is http://www.ncecho.org, a website that links six hundred North Carolina museums, libraries, historic sites, and archives.

South Carolina

South Carolina Department of Parks, Recreation, and Tourism
1205 Pendleton Street, Suite 106
Columbia, SC 29201
888-88-PARKS or 803-734-0122
http://www.discoversouthcarolina.com
(You can request free highway maps and vacation planners—a great
resource!)

Ghost Walks & Theatre

Many of these cities offer ghost walks seasonally or year-round.
Charleston, South Carolina, for example, offers five ghost walks and
historic tours. Wilmington, North Carolina, offers a ghost walk and
a haunted pub crawl (for adults only). Georgetown, South Carolina,
offers a ghost trolley—however, there must be enough people in the
group, and it must be prearranged. Local historic groups sometimes
offer special ghost walks during October and during historic
celebrations. Reservations are advised for all ghost walks and special
seasonal events. For more information, contact the aforementioned
tourism resources.

Additionally, Ghosts & Legends Theatre (Barefoot Landing,
North Myrtle Beach, SC) offers a different concept in ghostly
amusement. "Come meet the locals" in this live action show where
ghosts tell their own stories as the theatre comes to life all around
you. Historical, educational, and chilling tales unfold in a classic
Southern plantation parlor—once you pass through its secret panel
entrance. Meet the famous pirate Blackbeard, survive a Category
4 hurricane with the help of the Gray Man, and learn why there's

plenty of reason to fear the boo hag. The theatre is open all year, with shows performed daily every half-hour. The owners also offer a nightly ghost walk through Barefoot Landing and an entertaining séance (adults only). For more information call 843-361-2700 or visit www.GhostShows.com.

If you enjoyed reading this book, here are some other books from Pineapple Press on related topics. For a complete catalog, visit our website at www.pineapplepress.com. Or write to Pineapple Press, P.O. Box 3889, Sarasota, Florida 34230, or call 1-800-PINEAPL (746-3275). Or visit our website at www.pineapplepress.com.

Best Ghost Tales of North Carolina and *Best Ghost Tales of South Carolina* by Terrance Zepke. The actors of Carolina's past linger among the living in these thrilling collections of ghost tales. Experience the chilling encounters told by the winners of the North Carolina "Ghost Watch" contest. Use Zepke's tips to conduct your own ghost hunt.

Coastal North Carolina. Terrance Zepke visits the Outer Banks and the upper and lower coasts to bring you the history and heritage of coastal communities, main sites and attractions, sports and outdoor activities, lore and traditions, and even fun ways to test your knowledge of this unique region. Includes more than 50 photos.

Coastal South Carolina. Terrance Zepke shows you historic sites, pieces of history, recreational activities, and traditions of the South Carolina coast. Includes recent and historical photos.

Ghosts of the Carolina Coasts by Terrance Zepke. Taken from real-life occurrences and Carolina Lowcountry lore, these thirty-two spine-tingling ghost stories take place in prominent historic structures of the region.

Lighthouses of the Carolinas by Terrance Zepke. Here is the story of each of the eighteen lighthouses that aid mariners traveling the coasts of North and South Carolina. Includes visiting information and photos.

Pirates of the Carolinas, Second Edition, by Terrance Zepke. Thirteen of the most fascinating buccaneers in the history of piracy, including Henry Avery, Blackbeard, Anne Bonny, Captain Kidd, Calico Jack, and Stede Bonnet.

For more information on Terrance Zepke's books and future projects, see www.terrancezepke.com.

CPSIA information can be obtained at www.ICGtesting.com
Printed in the USA
BVOW06s1320080615

403336BV00006B/5/P

9 781561 643363